MURDER POST-DATED

by the same author

DEATH AND THE DUTIFUL DAUGHTER
DEATH OF A HEAVENLY TWIN
KILLING WITH KINDNESS
NURSERY TEA AND POISON
DEATH OF A WEDDING GUEST
MURDER IN MIMICRY
SCARED TO DEATH
MURDER BY PROXY
MURDER IN OUTLINE
DEATH IN THE ROUND
THE MEN IN HER DEATH
HOLLOW VENGEANCE
SLEEP OF DEATH

MURDER POST-DATED

ANNE MORICE

St. Martin's Press
New York

Library of Congress Cataloging in Publication Data

Morice, Anne.
    Murder post-dated.

    I. Title.
PR6063.0743M85   1984   823'.914   83-19266
ISBN 0-312-55321-8

First published in Great Britain in 1983 by Macmillan London Limited

First U.S. Edition

10 9 8 7 6 5 4 3 2 1

ONE

The card told us only that Mrs Carrington would be At Home for Emily at 9 p.m. on Saturday, 25th May, when there would be supper and dancing and that we should address our reply to Sowerley Grange, near Storhampton, Oxfordshire. But Elsa had written half a dozen lines on the back, which I read aloud to Robin:

'Just wanted to assure you that you won't be letting yourselves in for any unpleasantness this time. The murder has already taken place and I am happy to say that it turned out not to be a murder, after all. So do hope you'll both be able to come.'

This struck me as a novel variation and I asked Robin, who, as well as being my husband, is a Chief Inspector in the C.I.D., whether he had come across anything of the kind in his experience.

'All the time,' he replied.

'Oh, really? So, after all, how little I know about crime!'

'I am talking of events which were either not criminal, or, if they were, never got into the records.'

'Such as?'

'There are two examples which spring to mind. One is where a death occurs and some spiteful person puts it around that it was murder or manslaughter, usually naming the deceased's marriage partner as the culprit. This sometimes gets to the point where an investigation has to be set up, occasionally a post mortem as well, all of which invariably proves beyond doubt that death was due to natural causes.'

'And the other kind?'

'Oh, that's when a murder probably was intended, but was so inexpertly carried out that the victim survived. So no charges are brought.'

'And, in cases of that sort, does the would-be murderer usually have another shot?'

'Yes, quite often. By the way, why is Elsa giving a party for Millie?'

'It's her birthday.'

'But it sounds like the kind of formal dinner-dance affair which Millie wouldn't be seen dead at. I was under the impression that her idea of a rollicking party was to gloom around on the floor, listening to records and drinking coke?'

'Well, no doubt, this one was Elsa's idea, although it doesn't sound quite in her line either. On the other hand, perhaps Millie is becoming conventional in her old age. She'll be eighteen, after all. Shall I accept?'

'Why not? I'm sure you want to go and Elsa will understand if circumstances beyond my control oblige me to drop out at the last minute.'

'But I don't fancy driving back to London on my own at three o'clock in the morning and I can't very well ask her to put me up for the night. She'll have dozens of Millie's friends camping out all over the house, as it is.'

'Then you could stay at Roakes with Toby. It's only eight miles away, so you should be able to manage it, providing you go easy on the champagne.'

'Not a bad idea, Robin. I'll ring him up right away and make provisional reservations for us both. I fact, if you've no objection, I might extend my own booking by an extra day or two. That's the week we start shooting the Oxford scenes, all straw boaters and lacy parasols. They've booked me into an hotel, but it would be much more fun to stay with Toby and get them to lay on a car and driver instead. I really would like to go to Millie's party and I'm also keen to find out which type of non-murder Elsa was talking about. If it's the second, it seems to me that, whatever she may say, there could well be more unpleasantness to come.'

'Oh, don't worry. From what I know of the people of Sowerley, this will turn out to be a much more complicated affair than either of my two run-of-the-mill offerings.'

6

TWO

There were over a hundred guests, most of them in their late teens. The rest fell into two categories, one consisting of friends of Elsa's son, Marcus Carrington, who was several years older than his sister, the other of her own contempories, who had been roped in to provide moral support, the last group being seated round three sides of a refectory table on a dais at one end of the marquee.

This arrangement, like the invitation card, was in sharp contrast to Elsa'a normally casual brand of hospitality, but I was unable to ask her whether it was for Millie's benefit, or whether she had been taking a course in social climbing. By the time I arrived she was tearing around in a frenzy, issuing commands and countermands to the hired staff and evidently on the verge of a nervous breakdown. Small wonder either, for, as Marcus confided in a muttered aside, the torrential rain which had fallen during the morning had not only brought down one section of the marquee, wrecking the most spectacular flower piece of all, but had also transformed the meadow which was doing duty as a car park into a slimy bog.

In addition to this, it had now turned out that the hem of Millie's dress, which measured approximately four miles, had to be turned up before she would consent to wear it, and some of the more raffish guests had started rolling up at five o'clock, apparently under the impression that their arrival was the signal for the party to begin.

Strictly speaking, I did not qualify for any of the three age groups, but Elsa tactfully explained that, since Robin and I were both strong on moral support, she had placed us with the senior citizens and I was now stuck with them, even though circumstances beyond his control had forced him to drop out at the last minute. One who, owing to circumstances beyond Elsa's control, had dropped in at the last minute was the man on my left, whose name, as I was able to ascertain by a discreet lean sideways, was James Megrar. He appeared to be about forty, large in personality, as well as girth and height, bursting with energy and with a fast and voluble way of speaking, as though there could never be enough time to say everything that needed to be said.

I could not use the opening gambit of asking him how he pronounced his unusual surname because, although having either not heard or instantly forgotten it, we had in fact been formally introduced during the run-up to dinner. However, it at once became evident that no gambits, opening or otherwise, were needed to get this one going and within five minutes I had learnt that until recently he had been a partner in a firm of landscape gardeners in Sussex, but had now set up on his own, with offices in Dedley, and that his principal pleasures in life were fishing and bird watching.

Nor were his interests by any means confined to these activities and, having established that I was indeed Theresa Crichton, the actress, he began firing questions at me about the economics of the theatre, most of which proved him to be better informed on the subject than I was myself. Nevertheless, he listened attentively to the answers, which is always flattering, and then responded with more questions, interlarded with anecdotes, which were not only funny, but, in two cases, new to me.

In other circumstances, I knew that I should be enjoying this rattling exchange, but after a while I found myself losing the thread and giving only random and inadequate replies. There were a number of reasons for this. One was that I had scarcely had a chance to swallow more than two mouthfuls of the first course and was already well behind with the second, which I was becoming afraid might at any moment be snatched away. Another was that the band had now gone into action and, although consisting of only three instruments, the amplification was so deafening that it was difficult to hear what my garrulous neighbour was banging on about. Most inhibiting of all was the fidgeting and throat clearing which had now started up on my right.

There had been no need to crane and peer at this one's place card, for I knew him of old and could have guaranteed that, in addition to the audible signs of disapproval, there was a good deal of facial twitching and compulsive palm rubbing going on as well. Both these tricks were much in evidence, even when he was not in a state of umbrage, which most of the time he was.

His name was Tim Macadam, the husband of a great friend of Elsa's, who always defended him by claiming that a heart of gold was beating away beneath the bitten-up exterior and by reminding me that his had been a sad and difficult life. The second I knew to be true, but had still to obtain proof of the first.

The same reservations applied to his wife, Louise, a dowdy and truculent woman, all too apt at telling people that she and Tim had no time for the theatre and did not own a television set, as though this was something to boast about. Once or twice while Mr Megrar was doing his best to monopolise my attention, I had caught her inimical eye fixed on me from across the table and it had told me plainly that I was displaying all the ill-bred exhibitionism she most deplored in people of my calling.

'Who's the pretty girl next to Marcus?' I asked Tim, having snatched the chance to make amends, when my other neighbour momentarily turned away to serve himself with ice cream and raspberry sauce.

'You mean the blonde one?' he asked, looking down at the table where this group was seated.

'No, although I can understand your thinking so because she must be easily the best looking female present, but that is my cousin Ellen. She is happily married now to someone called Jeremy Roxburgh, so she no longer ranks as a pretty girl in that sense. I was referring to the dark one, on whose every word Marc appears to be hanging.'

9

'There's a lot of it about this evening,' Tim remarked in an acid voice. 'Her name is Laycock, I can tell you that much. Amanda or Anthea, or something. Louise will know, if it's really important to you.'

'Oh, it is and I shall certainly ask her. I take a special interest in Marc and Millie, you know.'

'Indeed?'

'Yes, it dates from when I was about twelve and used to be their baby-sitter. It has coloured our relationship ever since. If you happen to know the feminine for avuncular, it will tell you what colour I am talking about.'

'I'm afraid not, but I think I take your meaning and it may interest you to know that the man at the head of this table is the girl's father.'

'Thank you,' I said, taking a closer look at him. 'I was wondering who Elsa had got to play host for her.'

He was middle-aged with white hair and noble features and he looked like a well-fed saint.

'If you were to ask me what he does for a living, I should say rural dean or actor.'

'Then you'd be wrong on both counts. He's a Harley Street consultant.'

'Oh, really? What do people consult him about?'

'Any number of things, I shouldn't wonder. The broad term is allergies. Quite a lucrative branch of the profession, I understand. You're not likely to kill the patient, not to cure him either.'

'So lots of money?'

'Oh, indeed! It is, as they say, no object.'

'And so good-looking! His daughter takes after him.'

'Think so? I can't say I'd noticed.'

'But you're not so curious about people as I am, are you, Tim?'

'I never met anyone who was,' he replied, scoring a point and looking smug about it.

Disregarding this, I continued with the questions.

'Do they live round here?'

'They do now. His mother owned a biggish house just outside the village and the family used to come for summer holidays, Christmas and so on. The old lady died a year or two ago and now they just keep a small flat in London and spend most of their time here. Might have something to do with the wife being an invalid, I daresay.'

'What's the matter with her? Not an allergy, presumably?'

'Couldn't tell you. Louise would know.'

'Is she bedridden?'

'No, not as bad as that, but she hardly leaves the house and she has to have a nurse to look after her nowadays.'

This reminded me of something and I became silent and thoughtful, which was a mistake, because James Megrar seized his chance and came crashing into the attack again. Fortunately, the topic this time was books, in particular one he was currently reading about Marin County, which he found uproarious. Since I had not read it and his aim was evidently to make it unnecessary for me to do so, I was able to finish up the ice cream, without having to utter a word.

He was still in full spate when Elsa gathered up the female contingent and led us back to the house, another uncharacteristic formality, but one which had my approval for a change, because the tables in the centre of the marquee were now being stacked away, to provide a space for dancing. This had given rise to the irrational terror that Tim might feel a duty to invite me to stumble round the floor with him and the prospect would have been just as bleak if James Megrar had got in first. If his dancing had proved to be as energetic and uninhibited as his conversation, we should have been a menace to everyone else on the floor.

'Oh, hallo!' I said, when the moment had come for joining the ladies and he seated himself beside me. 'It is a pleasure to see you because it gives me the chance to congratulate you on having such a beautiful daughter. What is her name?'

'Yes, she is rather lovely, isn't she? Always has been since the day she was born. A sad day for me, but a joyous one too.

11

She is called Andrea.'

'Andrea Laycock. That goes very well. Mine is Theresa Crichton, by the way.'

'I know, I've been making enquiries and I shall now return the compliment by telling you how much I'm enjoying your television serial. I should hate to think of myself getting to the stage of turning down a social engagement for the sake of watching something on the box, but I have to confess that it's always a relief to find myself without one on Wednesday evening.'

I considered this to be charmingly put and told him so, adding, at the risk of appearing insatiable:

'Does Andrea watch it too? One always hopes the thing will appeal to all generations.'

'Oh yes, I believe so, from time to time, you know. She's out a good deal these days, but I gave her one of those video toys. I am not sure how often she uses it, to be perfectly honest.'

'And your wife? I imagine she watches a lot of television, since I hear she's an invalid?'

'Who told you that?' he asked, not, to be fair, clattering his cup against the saucer, but setting it down a little clumsily, so that some of the coffee slopped out.

'There now, how tiresome! I shall go and fetch myself a clean cup and saucer and some more coffee. May I refill yours?'

'No thanks, I still have some.'

I was not to know whether he had genuinely intended to return because, in any case, the decision was taken out of his hands. James Megrar came bounding across to fill the vacuum left by his departure and to ask me what I knew about witchcraft.

The truthful answer, which I gave him, was nothing at all and I could have added that I had confidently expected to get through life in the same state of ignorance, but he was not having any of that. I no longer remember how he came to be so well informed on the subject, although I believe it had

12

something to do with researching for a friend who was writing a book on the supernatural, but most of what he told me was so weird and incredible that I would have suspected him of making it up, had I not learnt that the more improbable a story, the more likely it is to be true.

None of the other guests ventured near us and I daresay he would have gone on all night, if I had been prepared to listen, but after almost an hour of it I told him that the time had come for me to seek out Jeremy, who had promised to take me home the minute I was ready to leave.

'He and my cousin Ellen and I are all staying with her father at Roakes Common,' I explained, 'and Jeremy is our chauffeur.'

His response to this was to offer to drive me home himself, saying that if I did not mind hanging on for another ten minutes, he would squelch through the mud and bring his car up to the front door. However, I decided that I had had enough entertainment and instruction for one evening and should stick to the original plan, making a passing reference to this, when I went over to take my leave of Elsa.

'I am relieved to hear it,' she said. 'Come and have lunch with me tomorrow and I'll explain.'

'I can't tomorrow, Elsa. Robin's hoping to get down for the day. I could manage Monday, though, if that's any good? We're shooting in Oxford all next week, but they don't need me on Monday.'

'Better still. I'll be on my own by then and there is much to report.'

'And much I want to hear,' I assured her.

THREE

'Tell me about Marc's new girl friend,' I said on Sunday morning, wondering how Ellen still managed to look like the fairy on the Christmas tree, after a gruelling evening and only five hours sleep. Long flaxen hair, large blue eyes and half an inch of black lashes no doubt got her off to a good start, but there was more to it than this. It was the serenity of her personality which made her shine like a good deed in a naughty world.

'Oh, she's all right, I suppose.'

'Coming from you, that sounds bad. What's the matter with her?'

'Nothing much and she's so beautiful. She just struck me as being a bit silly and conceited. I don't understand Marc, you know, Tessa. Jeremy tells me he's so jolly bright, but he's certainly no judge of women. Do you remember that last horror?'

'Who could ever forget her? But she was so cunning and deceitful. Andrea doesn't look that type.'

'No, but we were upstairs powdering our noses at one point and there was a queue for the bathroom, so I was stuck with her for about ten minutes. She was showing off like mad and she never stopped staring at herself in the glass for a single minute.'

'What kind of showing off?'

'Well, it was unbelievable really, because I hardly know her, but she kept on about how she wouldn't say this to anyone else, but she could tell instinctively that I was terribly discreet. I suppose she must have been a bit high, actually, that's the only way to account for it, because she didn't seem to notice that there were about five other women in the room as well. Either that, or she could tell instinctively

14

that they were deaf mutes. For all she knew, they could have been lapping up every word.'

'Every what word?'

'Well, it was mostly about her stepmother, who she can't stand, apparently.'

'Stepmother, did you say?'

'That's right. Why?'

'Oh, just trying to get the picture. Isn't she an invalid?'

'According to Andrea, that's just the cover story. The true one is that she's always been neurotically jealous, specially of Andrea, and it's now got to the stage where she's practically raving mad.'

'Does she have delusions that someone has been trying to kill her?'

'Honestly, Tessa, no wonder some people say you're a witch! However do you do it?'

'Not by supernatural means, I assure you. Was I right?'

'No, not quite. As a matter of fact, you got it completely back to front.'

'Oh well, that makes everything quite clear.'

'Andrea suffers from delusions that her stepmother is trying to kill someone.'

'Oh well, yes, I see what you mean. There is a subtle difference. Who was the intended victim?'

'All three of them. Her husband, Andrea and herself as well. There was some story about Andrea finding her mooning about in one of the sheds, with a tin of rat poison in her hand and the next evening they all had violent symptoms of food poisoning. Gregory was the worst, but he refused to call a doctor and she thinks this was because he'd guessed what had caused it and was afraid there might be some official enquiry, when it would all come out. Mind you, I don't believe a word of it. She must either be a compulsive liar, or she was a lot more drunk than she looked.'

'Drunk or not, do you honestly mean that she told you all this in a roomful of people?'

'Well, to be fair, I think most of them had gone by the time

15

we reached the climax because I remember being so relieved to see the bathroom was free at last and I could escape.'

'Don't tell me you just walked away at an exciting moment like that, without waiting to hear if there was more to come?'

'I didn't believe her, you see, and it wasn't worth the risk of losing my turn in the bathroom.'

'So that was the end of it, so far as you were concerned?'

'Yes. When I came out, she was so taken up with staring at her own face that she didn't notice me and I bolted downstairs. One thing I will tell you, though.'

'What?'

'I just hope Marc isn't getting too serious about her, because I have a feeling she could be very bad news.'

FOUR

True to her word, Elsa was alone when I arrived at Sowerley Grange, Marcus having returned to his chambers in London and Millie to her secretarial college.

'Are you still clearing up after the party?' I asked her.

'No, all done. The caterers were marvellous, well worth the expense. They packed everything up and on Sunday morning two lorries came and took it all away.'

'Well, it was a great triumph and I hope Millie was suitably grateful?'

'Oh, I think so. I think she enjoyed it in the end, despite all the grumbling that went on beforehand.'

'So it was your idea to give a great big show-off party?'

'Not exactly, no. It was really Marc who insisted on all the trappings. He's always been conventional, you know, and becoming more so, now that he's a fully fledged barrister.'

'And bent on forcing you and Millie into the same mould?'

'This time I suspect it was because he didn't want us to be shamed in the eyes of his new girl friend. Gregory Laycock has a very good opinion of himself, you know, and tends to take the attitude that the young man has yet to be born who is good enough for his daughter. Anyway, I didn't think it would hurt to indulge Marc, for once.'

'For once? You've been doing it since the day he was born.'

'That is quite untrue, Tessa. Apart from anything else, he never had a party of his own when he was Millie's age. It was too soon after his father died for any of us to have the heart for it. Besides, he went half shares in this one, so it was only fair he should have a say in the arrangements. What did you make of Gregory?'

'Didn't have much chance to study him. A bit flowery and

17

pompous, I thought. What did he mean by saying that the day Andrea was born was a sad one for him, but joyous as well?'

'I suppose he was referring to the fact that his first wife died in childbirth. It has been suggested that he married for the second time more to provide a substitute mother for Andrea than a wife for himself. If so, it doesn't appear to have worked out very successfully.'

'Well, I want to hear all about the Laycocks in a minute, but before we really get started on them, do fill me in about the man you put me next to at dinner.'

'James McGrath?'

'Oh, is that how you pronounce it?'

'How else?'

'God knows, but I've never seen that name spelt MEGRAR before.'

'Oh, that's just Millie. I was in a hurry and I asked her to do a new place card. She wants to do a course in journalism when she's learnt how to type, but her spelling is appalling. I do hope it won't be a drawback.'

'On the contrary, she'll be immune to misprints. Why were you so set against Mr McGrath driving me home? He's not a sex maniac, by any chance?'

'No, I have never heard that said about him, but he's not very popular with the people round here.'

'That might be because they suspect him of being more entertaining and better informed than they are, if you'll forgive my saying so. At any rate, that's how he struck me.'

'As we all noticed, and that's part of the trouble. He's so boastful and full of himself; always holding forth at such length about his bird watching and all the rest of it, which most of them aren't remotely interested in. That's why I only invited him, as a last resort, when Robin had to let me down. Nowadays, when people find themselves at a party with him, you can sense them watching him. It's as though they were waiting for him to commit some gaffe, so that they could rush to the telephone and tell all their friends about it as soon as

18

they got home. I didn't want your name to be bandied about in that sort of tittle-tattle.'

'Thank you, Elsa, and now that you've explained all that, let's move on to the Laycocks. Do you approve of Andrea?'

'Oh yes; considering how ridiculously her father spoils her, she's a very sweet girl.'

'Is that what they call accepting the inevitable gracefully?'

'Why do you say that?'

'There is something about the phrase "sweet girl", which is so damning, specially coming from you.'

'It wasn't intended to be, so I'll put it another way: she is beautiful, has good manners, I know nothing against her and, since Marc is obviously smitten, it is not for me to dig below the surface for hidden faults. My only worry is whether she is half as much in love with him as he is with her, which I sometimes doubt; and, even if she is, whether Gregory won't somehow contrive to break it up. I suppose it comes from his having been a single parent since the day of Andrea's birth, but he really does seem to be quite exaggeratedly possessive about her. However, that's something they'll all have to work out for themselves.'

'Right! So now you can tell me about your murder which turned out not to be one, after all. Would I be right in assuming that it involved the Laycocks in some way?'

'Good gracious, no. Really, Tessa, you do pick up some extraordinary ideas! I wonder where you got hold of this one?'

'Not from anywhere in particular. I know very little about them, but I have been made aware of a certain mystery surrounding Mrs Laycock. I admit it occurred to me that the word might have got around that someone had it in for her, or else that she wasn't ill, but mentally deranged and so had to be kept in the charge of a wardress disguised as a nurse. In other words, that she had to be protected from making another attempt to kill herself or someone else.'

'You have a vivid imagination and I am afraid it has led you astray this time. So far as I am aware, neither story has ever been circulated. I was referring to an altogether different scandal, concerning quite a different wife.'

'Anyone I know?'

'You know the husband. You met him here on Saturday.'

'You wouldn't be referring to James McGrath!'

'Yes, I would.'

'There now! I was off the mark, wasn't I? What happened to his wife?'

'She disappeared.'

'So everyone said he'd killed her and then she spoilt all the fun by turning up again, alive and kicking? Although she wasn't at your party, obviously.'

'No, and the story wasn't quite as tame as that, either.'

'Good! Tell me how it did turn out.'

'Her name is Rosamund. She is about the same age as him and reputed to have most of the money. She is a nice woman, a shade too reserved for my taste, but always pleasant and civil, if you know what I mean?'

'And therefore more popular than her husband, presumably?'

'Which is precisely why we were all so puzzled when she disappeared like that, without a word to anyone, not even ringing up to say goodbye. Tim and Louise, who are their nearest neighbours, were away at the time, spending the weekend at some hotel they go to every year in the Lake District. When they got back Rosamund had gone. No message, nothing.'

'And so, of course, they immediately assumed that her husband had killed her and buried the remains in the garden?'

'Not at first, that came later. To begin with, we all accepted his explanation without question.'

'Which was?'

'That her cousin Isobel had been taken seriously ill and that Rosamund was staying up in London, so as to be near the hospital. We all knew that she was devoted to this cousin. She was an orphan and Isobel's parents had brought her up, so they were more like sisters. It was quite a reasonable story and he might have got away with it, for a while at any rate.'

'What went wrong?'

'Unfortunately for him, Louise, who was more friendly with Rosamund than most of us, was in London herself only a few days later. She'd met Isobel before and she happened to run into her in Knightsbridge. She was in excellent health and she hadn't seen or heard from Rosamund for months. You can imagine how that set all the tongues wagging? Mine as much as anyone else's, I'm ashamed to say.'

'And did any of them go wagging to the police?'

'I believe so: She denied it later, but I have an idea that Louise . . . well, anyway, if so, there was evidently nothing they could do about it. Rosamund hadn't been reported as missing and there was no dead body, so presumably no justification for interfering. Just as well, too, because when the entire neighbourhood had been humming with sinister rumours for over a week, we heard the true explanation.'

'I hope it won't be too much of an anti-climax?'

'Knowing Rosamund, or rather believing we knew her, all of us found it sensational enough, but I daresay you won't. She'd run away with another man.'

'No, honestly? How did you find out?'

'From two sources, Louise being the intermediary in both.'

'She is a busy woman, that Louise, isn't she?'

'Well, as I told you, she and Rosamund were friends and near neighbours, so it was natural for her to play a more active part in the affair than someone like myself, for instance. Obviously, she was worried when she discovered that the story about the cousin being ill was untrue and, when still nothing was heard from her, Louise nerved herself to go and see James and warn him that she didn't intend to let him get away with the deception any longer.'

'And how did he react to that?'

'It completely took the wind out of his sails, I gather. He broke down and admitted that Rosamund had left him for another man. He didn't know his name, or anything about him, but she had left a note, saying she'd fallen in love with someone else who she thought she could be happy with, that she'd be in touch with him when they'd both had a chance to adjust to the situation. James, however, feels certain that she'll think better of it and come back to him. He told Louise that was why he'd invented the story about her cousin. If and when she did come back, he didn't want it known that she'd ever left him. He begged Louise not to spread it around and she gave him her word that she wouldn't.'

'But her word was not her bond?'

'Oh yes, it was. She played absolutely fair, but what happened was that only a few days later she had a letter from Rosamund herself. It covered much the same ground, but there was nothing about its being confidential, so Louise felt she was no longer under any obligation to keep silent about it.'

'Goodness, what an exciting time it must have been! When did all this happen?'

'Five or six weeks ago.'

'And nothing has been heard from her since?'

'Not as far as I know.'

'And you still have no idea who she went off with?'

'None whatever. It can't have been anyone local, or we'd certainly have heard by now. What a dark horse she was, under that shy and diffident exterior! The theory now is that half the time when she was reputed to be staying either with her cousin in London, or else with friends in Sussex, she was actually with this man, although who he was and where they met is still a mystery. Anyway, the sensation has died a natural death now. Perhaps it would get a revival if she should come back, as James still feels confident that she will. Anyway, you can see now why I made my little joke about the murder which turned out not to be one?'

'I wouldn't be too sure of that, Elsa, if I were you.'

'Oh, really, Tessa, you're incorrigible! Haven't I just told you that Louise had a letter from Rosamund, written in her own hand and repeating in almost the same words what she'd already heard from James?'

'Which is precisely what strikes me as dubious.'

'For goodness sake, why?'

'I wouldn't have expected her to express herself to Louise in identical terms to those she had used in a letter to be seen only by her husband.'

'Oh, that's just a quibble.'

'And here comes another! How well does Louise know Rosamund's handwriting?'

'As well as one knows any of one's friends', I suppose.'

'I was just thinking that, as these particular friends presumably lived within half a mile of each other . . .'

'Closer than that, as it happens. The McGraths bought Orchard House, which, as you'll remember, is only just down the road from the Macadams.'

'Then I assume they would have communicated mainly by telephone?'

'Oh yes, mainly, of course they would, but there are always occasions for writing, aren't there? Notes left on the kitchen table when Louise was out, or to say thank you for a party. Postcards when she went away on holiday, all that kind of thing.'

'I suppose so. Tell me more about the letter, though. Obviously, there was no address, but did it give any clue at all as to where she had gone?'

'No. It had a London postmark, but that means nothing. She could easily have arranged for it to be posted by someone she could trust not to give her away.'

'Did Louise show it to you?'

'Yes, she did. It was a curious sort of letter, in a way. I remember thinking she must have written it in a hurry because it was quite short and it had no beginning.'

'How can one write a letter, however short, without beginning it?'

'No introduction is what I meant. It just went straight into "I want to try and make you understand, etc., etc.".'

'Honestly, Elsa, you amaze me sometimes.'

'What have I said now?'

'You're so trusting! How could you fail to see through a trick like that?'

'So simple minded, I suppose you mean? Are you suggesting it was a forgery?'

'Of course, I am. I should have thought it was obvious.'

'But I keep telling you that Louise recognised the handwriting.'

'I know you do and I daresay it was a good enough imitation to get by, so long as there was nothing to compare it with, and was there? The sort of notes and cards you mentioned are not likely to be filed away for future reference; but what clinches it for me is that missing introduction.'

'I don't see why.'

'Because including one could have been a dead give-away. Some women sprinkle "darlings" and "dearests" about in conversation like sugar on the strawberries, but they don't necessarily use them in correspondence. And vice versa, of course. Louise would have noticed at once if the opening endearment had been too effusive or too impersonal, so clever Mr Forger played safe and omitted it altogether.'

'You do realise, of course, that if by some incredible chance you were right, there is only one person who could have done it?'

'You mean James McGrath? Yes, and I consider he has been very intelligent about it.'

'I can't say I agree with you.'

'Well, the way I see it is this: a less astute man, having murdered his wife and buried her corpse in the garden, would doubtless have given it out that she had left him and run off with someone else, which would inevitably have given rise to endless gossip and speculation, the last thing he wanted. You agree?'

'Yes, I daresay it would. In fact, it did, but I still can't see why telling two separate lies was so much cleverer than finding one good one and sticking to it. Why make it so complicated?'

'Well, you see, Elsa, the first one, the one about the dying cousin, served a double purpose. He would have realised, of course, that it wouldn't hold up for long, but it gave him a breathing space, time to manoeuvre outside the glare of the limelight. Then, in due course, Louise turns up, breathing fire and brimstone, and he is able to use that first lie as proof of how grief-stricken he is, how he's praying his wife will return and that no one will find out that she left him, thereby neatly spiking Louise's guns. Faced with that confession, even she might be expected to feel ashamed of herself. So then, when the forged letter arrived, there was a good chance she would hold her tongue. It might occur to her that she was becoming paranoiac on the subject and, in any case, she would have hesitated to go into battle again and risk making an utter fool of herself, if the letter did prove to be genuine. I think he sized her up correctly, too, and that's exactly what did happen. If you ask me, that's why she showed it to you.'

'To see whether I would notice any flaws in it?'

'Exactly! And when you didn't she probably thought that was good enough. At any rate, she decided not to go it alone.'

'There are times, you know, Tessa, when it saddens me that someone so fundamentally kind and good-natured as you are should have such a suspicious mind. Still, there it is and you've been vindicated often enough in the past, so I suppose you could be right this time. What do you advise me to do about it?'

'Why do anything? It's not really your business.'

'Oh, I don't think I could just drop it and pretend to go on in blissful ignorance, now that you've pointed out what wickedness may lie behind it. I'm afraid I shall have to ask Louise straight out whether she's truly satisfied that the letter was genuine. Why don't we go together, this very afternoon? Then she can show it to you.'

'Oh no, Elsa, I'm sure that would be fatal. The mere sight of me brings Louise out in a rash and she'd shut up like a clam.'

25

'On the contrary. I know you two have a way of bringing out the worst in each other, but she has great respect for your intelligence. She's often told me so.'

'Something tells me I have a better chance of keeping her respect if I also keep my distance. Besides, I can't go this afternoon, I've promised to spend a little time with Ellen. They were out to dinner last night, so I've hardly seen her and we couldn't talk this morning because she and Jeremy were both in floods of tears.'

'Oh dear, why was that?'

'Because Jeremy has to go to Geneva for forty-eight hours.'

'Why doesn't she go with him, if parting is so painful?'

'She did once, but she found Geneva very boring when Jeremy was immured behind steel doors, talking to bankers for most of the day. Also it would mean sacrificing the blissful reunion on Wednesday evening. But do ring up and let me know how you got on with Louise.'

'Oh, I will and I just hope and trust that this time you'll be proved wrong.'

'Cheer up!' I said. 'It has been known.'

FIVE

Toby and Ellen were having tea by the swimming pool and when she had fetched an extra cup from the kitchen Ellen launched into a detailed description of a film which she and Jeremy had seen the night before in Storhampton.

Toby kept cutting in with remarks like: 'Dear me, how dreadfully uninteresting!' but it did not discourage her and she ploughed relentlessly on until he was obliged to do what he would have done in the cinema, which was to walk out.

'What's got into you?' I asked her.

'Yes, sorry about that, but I had to find some way to drive him indoors because I want to tell you the latest about Andrea.'

'And it's not fit for Toby's ears?'

'Oh yes, but he'd have kept interrupting to ask us whether we thought it was a situation he could use. It would have taken the whole afternoon to argue that out and I have to go back to London in a minute.'

I took her meaning. Toby earns his living by writing plays, but the living is not quite as good as it ought to be because he is so lazy about it and always hoping other people will do half the work by providing him with plots, which they very rarely do.

'Just as well he went when he did too,' Ellen added, 'because I was running out of steam. We all left before the end, you won't be surprised to hear.'

'All?'

'Yes, Marc and Andrea came with us and afterwards we went to have dinner at that new restaurant in the Market Place. As soon as we got there Andrea and I made a dash for the Ladies and that's when she started on about her stepmother again.'

'Lavatories do seem to bring out that certain streak in

her.'

'Well, this was slightly different. She admitted that she'd had too much to drink at the party and, although she couldn't remember much about it the next day, she had a ghastly feeling that she'd given me a lot of yackety-yack about her stepmother.'

'So she was retracting?'

'Yes, she was, but I'll tell you something funny, Tessa. You know how I said I didn't believe her the first time? Well, the funny part is that I didn't believe her the second time either.'

'That must have taken some doing?'

'Not really, because I'm sure I'd have gone on disbelieving the first story, if only she hadn't denied it. Now I begin to wonder if it was a case of *in vino veritas*.'

'Why?'

'Well, for one reason, because she asked me if I'd repeated it to Jeremy and when I said no, instead of looking relieved, as you'd expect, she looked . . . well, more like disappointed. Also I'm not convinced that people do tell outrageous lies when they're stoned. I think they're more likely to tell outrageous truths and then wish to God they hadn't.'

'Unless they happen to be compulsive liars, which at the last hearing was your verdict on Andrea.'

'And we don't like that any better, do we? It may be some comfort to know that there isn't a murderess in the family, but the alternative would seem to be that Marc had fallen for a nutcase. Take your pick!'

Before I could so do, Toby came ambling across the grass to tell me that I was wanted on the telephone.

'You took your time,' Elsa said, sounding as cross as two sticks about it.

'Not my fault. You ought to know by now that Toby doesn't relay such messages at the gallop.'

'I do know and it wasn't that which made me irritable. I just wish so much that you hadn't got me involved in this

28

business of Rosamund's letter.'

'You tackled Louise, then?'

'This afternoon, as soon as you left. I wanted to get it over. And you were right, of course. She simply pounced on it when I told her I'd been thinking it over and been wondering if there could be anything spurious about it. She agreed at once, but said that she'd kept quiet about it for fear of influencing me, because the last thing she wanted was to stir up trouble, if there was no reason to.'

'Oh, yes?'

'Now, Tessa, I know you don't like her, but she's not a mischief-maker and her concern is purely altruistic.'

'If you say so, Elsa. What's the next move, then?'

'Well, the first thing, of course, is to consult Tim, when he gets home this evening. Then, if he approves, she'll telephone the police station tomorrow and make an appointment to see the Superintendent. Naturally, she wants me to go too, to back her up and, having made the first move, I hardly see that I can refuse.'

'Yes, and I'm very sorry to have brought it on you.'

'Well, that's spilt milk now and we must look at it from a practical point of view. What I want you to tell me is whether you think the Superintendent will take it seriously and, if so, what he's likely to do about it.'

'I can't answer either question with any certainty, but at a guess I should say that he'll have no choice. Even if he privately thought it was a storm in a teacup and that you were just a couple of hysterical women with a grudge against James McGrath, he'd be bound to take it a step or two further.'

'And what will that mean?'

'Still guessing, I'd say that he'll find some means of getting hold of a genuine specimen of Rosamund's handwriting and then send the whole lot off to be compared by experts. That could well be the end of it.'

'And if not?'

'You can do your own guessing there, surely?'

'Yes, and I just pray with all my heart that a storm in a teacup is what it will turn out to be. I shan't know a moment's peace until I hear.'

'Well, try not to worry too much because there's a good chance your prayer will be answered and the worst you'll have to suffer is to go down in police records as a relatively harmless lunatic.'

'Thanks very much, Tessa. You're a great comfort, I must say.'

I helped Ellen to carry the luggage out to her car, waved goodbye to her as she bucketed along over the Common, then went back indoors again to ask Toby if he would mind being left on his own for an hour or so, as I had an act of penance to perform.

'I daresay the time will swish by like lightning,' he replied, 'but please try not to be late for dinner. Mrs Parkes is making a seafood platter and we are expected to be sitting up in our chairs by eight o'clock sharp.' Seafood platter used to be known as grilled sole, but her vocabulary has changed out of all recognition since she and Parkes went on a package holiday to Florida.

Orchard House had also undergone a sea change since my last visit. In those days, owing to the poverty and fecklessness of the tenants, it had been notable for its shabby and derelict appearance. Now all was newly painted and in good repair and the garden presented an even more dramatic transformation. Gone were the spindly, gnarled old apple trees, the patch of waste ground covered with plantains and buttercups which had passed as a lawn, and the waist-high weeds in what had once been flower beds. In their place were dozens of sturdy saplings, half an acre of newly-laid turf and three or four half-moon shaped beds, ablaze with herbaceous plants and roses.

It should have been a sight to gladden the heart and eye, but there was something spooky about it as well, and it did not take long to pinpoint the reason for this. Between the lawn and the orchard there was roughly a quarter of an acre of land which had evidently been designated as the kitchen garden. It had been marked out into four large, rectangular beds, bordered and separated from each other by brick paths. Spade work was literally still in progress on this section, two of the beds having been dug and spread with compost, the third half completed and the remaining one still in its virgin state. It caused quite a frisson to realise how soon and for what purpose these freshly-dug beds might soon all be dug up again.

I had not yet fully made up my mind to take the plunge and ring the doorbell and had been half hoping that, were I to summon the nerve to do so, there would be no one at home to answer it. There was, though, and he must have spied me from a window because, as I stood hesitating beside the white painted wooden gate, the front door opened and he came out on to the porch and shouted at me to come inside. When I obeyed, he led the way to the kitchen, where, as he explained, he was sloshing through a backlog of washing-up.

'Ran out of powder,' he explained, correctly interpreting my glance at the dishwasher. 'My wife's away, you see, and I'm not very well organised. Domesticity is one of the talents I still have to acquire. We do have a daily, although that's boasting a bit. She's more what you'd call a once-a-weekly. Now, what shall I give you by way of a drink?'

Still talking, he fetched glasses from one cupboard, bottles from another and set them out on the table, and the weird part of it was that he never once asked me why I had come, seeming to regard it as the most natural thing in the world that I should have dropped in uninvited.

However, I was determined not to leave him with any illusions for longer than was necessary and, at the first break in the flow, I said:

'I am afraid I bring bad news.

He did not drop the bottle he was pouring from, nor clatter it against the glass, but for once he was stopped in his tracks and a full half minute went by before he responded. Then, speaking in exactly the same tone as before, he said:

'Well now, and what would someone like you be bringing me bad news about?'

'I think you may be in for some trouble and I felt it was only fair to come and warn you because the horrid truth is that it is I who am responsible.'

'I find that hard to believe.'

'You won't, when you've heard,' I assured him and then repeated everything Elsa had told me about Rosamund's disappearance, as well as everything I had said to her in reply and concluding with her latest telephone call.

He listened to the end, without a single interruption, which was unexpected enough, but there seemed to be no limit to his capacity to spring surprises, for when I had finished speaking he pushed back his chair and stood up, saying:

'There now, you had me so engrossed I forgot all about ice. I am sure your drink would taste better for it?'

'No, please don't bother, it's fine as it is. I hope you're not going to probe too deeply into my motives for advising her as I did,' I went on when he had sat down again. 'I'm afraid they're not so righteous and disinterested as I should like them to be. Something to do with vanity, I suppose. You know, trying to be clever? And when I get carried away on that game I tend to forget that there are human beings involved.'

'It happens to all of us, from time to time.'

'In my own defence, I'd like you to know that I did make some attempt to pull back right at the end and to persuade Elsa that there was no call for her to take any action, but of course it was too late by then. I had sown the wind, as a friend of mine used to say. However, it's a relief to find that you don't seem too bothered about it.'

'No, I'm not. In fact, all self-recrimination can now cease because, in a way, I'm grateful to you.'

'Then you must be a most unusual man.'

'You only feel that because I sometimes have a different way of looking at things from most people's and the difference now is that I am seeing further ahead than you are.'

'And what does that show you?'

'Not having seen the letter, I am unable to say whether it is a forgery or not, but one thing I do know. So long as there's a single friend of Rosamund's who believes that it is and so long as she stays away it will go on festering like an ulcer, and you know what will happen then? Some day it will flare up and it will take a major operation to put things right again. The best way to deal with it is for the forces of law and order to take over. If they don't manage to nip it in the bud, at least they'll make a tidy job of it.'

'That's true, I suppose.'

'You may be sure it is, and there's something more I can tell you to cheer you up. If they do take over, it may even lead to their finding out where Rosamund is and that wouldn't be bad either. It would solve a few of my own problems, if nothing else. So there we are! All in all, you've done me a good turn, so why don't we both have another drink to celebrate?'

'I'd like to, but I can't stop any longer. I have strict orders not to be late for dinner. Also I have to be up and about with a clear head by seven in the morning.'

'Make it another time, then. And thanks for coming!'

'What you could describe as a slippery customer,' Toby remarked, when we had scraped up the last of the seafood platter, and I had brought him up to date with the latest development. 'You think he was bluffing?'

'I couldn't tell you whether he was or not, but, if so, he made a good job of it. He's either a cartload of monkeys, or just a decent man whose manners don't happen to recommend themselves to the society he finds himself in.'

'Yes, and why does he find himself in it, I wonder? What does this neighbourhood have to offer that he couldn't find in

33

Sussex? Could it be that the garden of Orchard House was in such urgent need of a good dig?'

'No, I must say I doubt whether Rosamund lies buried under the new rose bushes. Whatever else, he's no fool. But please don't forget, Toby, that when the telephone rings tomorrow it could be Elsa, who's forgotten that I shall be working. So don't fail to answer it yourself and take careful note of everything she says. And now I shall go to bed because I'm worn to a shred. My goodness, who would ever imagine that this was supposed to be my day of rest?'

SIX

It was lucky that I should have been hovering in the hall at seven o'clock the next morning and thus able to pick up the telephone on the first ring. Otherwise one can never be sure that conscience wouldn't have compelled Toby to get out of bed and answer it himself. This would have been a double annoyance for him, since the caller was not Elsa, but Ellen.

'I wanted to catch you before you left,' she explained.

'And you have succeeded, though only just. What's so urgent?'

'I wondered whether it would be okay to bring Andrea over to Oxford to watch you at work?'

'Yes, I should think so. I'll fix it with Jean. We're doing a river scene this morning, so it may have its comical moments, if nothing else. Whose idea was this?'

'Andrea's. I'd mentioned the film to her on Sunday evening and last night she rang up to ask if there was any chance I'd be able to wangle it. Apparently, she's mad keen to get into television herself.'

'My God, there seems to be no end to this girl's flights of fancy. Still, hanging about for three hours, watching them do the same shot fourteen times over, may cure her of that particular ambition.'

'I doubt it, and what she'd really like is for us all to have lunch together, so that she can talk to you about it. I promised to ask you, because it will give you a chance to study her in close-up and see if you agree with me that Marc needs rescuing.'

'Oh, all right, but I hope you warned her that it will only be a canteen lunch and that the dining room is a converted bus. Listen, Ellen, I've got to ring off because I can see the car coming. We'll be in the meadow just below Magdalen

Bridge. You can't miss it.'

She looked even more spectacular at close quarters than from a distance, having been blessed with the striking combination of black hair and violet blue eyes. She had also spent some time highlighting these and other features with almost as much expertly applied make-up as if she had come prepared to spend the day in front of the cameras, instead of several yards behind them. It made me wonder whether she could really be so naïve as to imagine that the way to break into television was to catch the eye of the director, who would instantly gallop over to offer her a part in his next production and, in fact, it turned out that she was.

'Ellen tells me that you'd like to work in the business yourself,' I said, when we had loaded our plates with roast lamb, two veg and all the trimmings. 'Is it acting or the production side which appeals to you?'

'Oh, acting, although I wouldn't mind starting off by learning to direct, or something, if you think that would be a good way to do it.'

I could hardly believe my ears. She not only had a tinny, affected little voice, which would have ruled out her chances as soon as she opened her mouth, but a tinny, addled little brain to go with it, if she expected such statements to be taken seriously.

'Have you had any experience?'

'Not a lot. I did a course in modelling a few years ago, so I know how to move well, which I'm told gives you a head start. And I've taken some singing lessons.'

'Not quite enough, perhaps?' Ellen suggested, without a smile.

I shook my head, not daring to speak, in case I should break into laughter.

'So what would you advise me to do, Tessa?'

'Well, look,' I said, making an effort to stay calm, 'I only have an hour for lunch and I'd need much longer than that to explain why it takes more than looks, and the ability to walk

36

across a room without knocking into anything, to break into television. There are dozens of professional actresses with all that and a lot more besides, who count themselves lucky to get three months work in a year. The only honest advice I can give you is to forget it and go for some slightly less over-crowded profession. However, if you're absolutely bent on going ahead, your only hope is to get some training. If you like, I'll give you an introduction to the principal of a drama school, who's an old friend of mine, and ask him to audition you.'

'Oh well, if you say so, I suppose I might as well.'

'I should warn you, however, that old friend notwithstanding, there's no guarantee that he'll give you an audition, still less that you'll get a place in the school, as a result. They have twenty times more applicants than they can accept.'

'Oh, but it's not as though I'd need a scholarship or anything. I'm sure Daddy would be perfectly willing to cough up the fees.'

'So would countless other Daddies with stage-struck daughters. The point is, Andrea, that this man couldn't care less about your financial assets. It's talent he'll be looking for.'

'So, in that case, I stand the same chance as everyone else?'

'Exactly the same chance and it's tiny. Sorry to sound so discouraging, but that's the way things are, so I'd give it some thought, if I were you. Now, eat up both of you, otherwise we shan't have time for the plums and custard.'

Two hours later, during a break between shots, while the cameras were being set up in new positions, Ellen came tripping up the steps of my mobile dressing-room.

'We're off now,' she said. 'I came to say goodbye and thank you.'

'If you ask me, that friend of yours has been off for years. Her head, I mean.'

'I did warn you.'

'Yes, you did, but I wasn't expecting her to be a complete

37

half-wit.'

'I must admit that I didn't realise either she was quite so ignorant and, if you'll forgive my saying so, Tessa, I think you handled it rather badly.'

'How could anyone be forgiven for saying that? And she'll have to get her feet down on the ground sooner or later. Someone was going to flatten her one day, so why not me?'

'Because I think, if you hadn't argued with her and taken it all so seriously, she'd most likely have forgotten about it in a day or two and moved on to some new fantasy. As it is, she's really got the bit between her teeth now. She probably thinks you were trying to put her off because you were afraid of the competition. Anyway, it's now become a challenge and she's determined to prove you wrong.'

'Oh well, fat lot I care! Let her go ahead and find out how it feels to get the real gilt-edged snub. At least, while it lasts she'll have less time for Marc, so perhaps we've done a good day's work there.'

'You may not have done yourself any good, though. I'll try and head her off, but just now she's all set to take you up on your offer to give her a letter of introduction.'

'Then she shall have it, plus a very special request to my poor old friend to do his best for her. Having met her, I think we'll be better off with an aspiring actress on our hands than an aspiring Mrs Marc Carrington.'

SEVEN

'Did anyone telephone?' I asked on Wednesday morning.

'Elsa, for one, as you predicted. I told her you'd be able to call her back some time around nine, but I was wrong.'

'Yes, I'm sorry I couldn't let you know I'd be late, but one of the sound crew has had a baby and he wanted to know if I'd be godmother. So of course I said yes and that led to a session at the pub and, one way and another, it turned into quite a convivial evening.

'Is that why you decided not to go to work this morning?'

'No, that's because they're doing some background shots in one of the quads and I'm not needed. I'm afraid it means you'll be lumbered with me for an extra day or two next week, if you can stand it, but in the meantime I have the whole day off and I'd better use some of it up by calling Elsa.'

'You won't be eating into it very deeply. She only wanted you to know that the policeman had kept the letter and had passed the remark that he would be looking into the matter.'

'Oh, I see! Poor Louise must have been very cast down by such a tepid reaction. Who else rang up?'

'Two others, starting with Andrea Laycock.'

'There now! So Ellen was right!'

'She very often is, I find. It is a pity, but perhaps she will grow out of it.'

'Did Andrea leave any message?'

'No, she said she would try again today. I told her there would be no use in her doing so before eight o'clock this evening. Wrong again!'

'Not your fault. Anyone else?'

'Your murderer friend.'

'James McGrath? What did he want?'

'To see you. I told him . . .'

'Yes, I can guess and, considering what a penance it is for you to answer even your own calls, you must have had a trying day. Did he say why he wanted to see me?'

'No, only that he hoped you would be able to have a drink with him this evening. You can see what that led me into? If you require me to act as your telephonist and social secretary, it might be as well to inform me of your movements in advance.'

'I didn't know myself until yesterday that the schedule had been changed. And I'm not sure that you did get the answer wrong that time.'

'So you won't feel like having a drink with him this, or any other evening? Perhaps you are wise. There could be an element of risk in it, I daresay.'

'It's not that which worries me so much. More of a reluctance to become any more embroiled in his affairs than I am already. On the other hand, I do feel rather guilty about landing him in this mess, in spite of his taking it so well. Or maybe because of that. It is rather hard to decide.'

'And I'm afraid I can't advise you. For one thing, I can't spare the time. My own schedule got badly upset yesterday, one way and another, and I must try and catch up with some work. You will have to sort it out for yourself.'

'Perhaps I should start by inviting myself to lunch with Elsa. I might manage to drag something slightly more illuminating out of her than she saw fit to divulge on the telephone. Mrs Parkes wasn't expecting me to be here, so at least her schedule won't be affected.'

'I really have no idea whether he meant to take it any further or not,' Elsa replied. 'He asked if we would mind having our fingerprints taken, but he didn't explain why. He was extremely cagey. I suppose they always are.'

'Besides which, he may not have known himself at that point whether he would make any move or not.'

'Oh, Tessa, surely?'

'Well, it's delicate, isn't it? I daresay he thought a

consultation with his Chief Constable might be in order, before plunging in up to his neck.'

'And what's his attitude likely to be?'

'Goodness knows, we'll have to wait and see. In the meantime, it may take your mind off that troublesome subject to learn that I am taking tea with the Laycocks this afternoon.'

'You are? How did that come about? I thought you told me you'd never met them before?'

I gave her an account of Andrea's visit to the film location, adding:

'Did you realise that she had ambitions to become an actress?'

'No, certainly not. Are you sure?'

'It is the reason why I have been invited to tea. I have been roped in to give some practical help in heaving her up the ladder to stardom.'

'How strange! Marc has never mentioned it.'

'I know that you like and approve of her, Elsa, but could it be that she is apt to fantasise a little, here and there?'

'Why do you say so?'

'Well, this dream of becoming a television star overnight doesn't exactly belong in the realms of realism, would you say?'

'Perhaps not, but a lot of girls go through that phase at one stage or another.'

'Ellen tells me she's twenty-six, so she's left it a bit late.'

'Well, I don't know, Tessa. I can only speak as I find, as the saying goes, and on the one or two occasions when Marc has brought her here, I have always found her perfectly normal and unassuming.'

'Perhaps that's another act, which she reserves specially for you? The well brought up, butter-wouldn't-melt daughter-in-law elect.'

'Not necessarily. People are rarely all of a piece and she would naturally present a different side of herself to someone of my generation. It doesn't follow that either is a sham.'

41

'And she certainly has a good many sides to present. Do you want to hear what reason she gave for inviting me to tea, instead of the conventional drink? It was so that there would be no risk of our being interrupted or overheard by her father, whom she has now discovered to be bitterly opposed to her taking up any sort of theatrical career. Can you believe it? Does there exist a father in this day and age with such a prejudice, or one who would dare to express it aloud, if he had?'

'I wonder you have allowed yourself to be caught up in this tangled web, if that's what you consider it to be?'

'I rashly offered to help her and now I'm stuck with it. Besides, I don't regard her as a liar in the accepted sense. I think she probably belongs in that tiresome grey area where every word becomes true as soon as it is uttered. Also, with any luck, I'll get a chance to meet the mysterious Mrs Laycock.'

'Honestly, Tessa, I cannot imagine where you pick up these extraordinary ideas. I hardly know the poor woman, no one does, except possibly Louise, but to the best of my knowledge she suffers from nothing more mysterious than chronic arthritis. She has to keep going into hospital for therapy and so on and when she's at home she's usually in so much pain that she very rarely goes out. At any rate, that's what I gather from Andrea.'

'Then it must be true,' I said, 'for where would you find a more reliable informant than her?'

'How did you get on?' Toby asked an hour or two later.

'Not at all well. In fact, it was a complete waste of time and I wasn't even offered a cup of tea.'

'Or a glimpse of Mrs Mystery?'

'No, she didn't appear and it's hard to understand why I was invited. Andrea has changed her mind since yesterday afternoon and the television industry now has to face the fact that it must struggle on without her.'

'Oh well, that should be a relief to you?'

'Yes and no.'

'Did she give you any reason?'

'Yes, and we must award her full marks there because it was a most noble and unselfish one. She had decided to sacrifice herself on the altar of her father's prejudice. I suppose that what actually happened is that she invented this tale of his objecting to her taking up acting, as a way out of it for herself. Then she decided to squeeze a bit more drama out of it and she needed an audience. It didn't stop there either. She tacked on some embroidery about his being so worried about his wife's mental condition that she felt it would be unkind to add to his anxieties. Which is why I'm not shouting for joy about having been let off so lightly. I'm thinking of Marc, you see. He's already been through one disasterous love affair and I'd hate to see him knocked flat on his face all over again, which is what Ellen and I are afraid will happen, if Andrea decides that marriage is where her true vocation lies.'

'Well, there's nothing you can do about it.'

'No, there isn't and it's a thoroughly depressing situation, topped off by a thoroughly wasted afternoon. How about yours? What have you been up to?'

'Answering your telephone calls, chiefly.'

'Oh, hell! Who from this time?'

'Robin, to say he can collect you from Oxford on Friday evening and spend the weekend here, if that suits us both. Your agent about an American television series, which she doesn't think you'll want to do because sixteen weeks in L.A. might put rather a strain on your marriage. On the other hand, I am to tell you that the part is right up your street, having to do with an English au pair girl with an all-American family. Also that the money is good.'

'Thank you. Anyone else?'

'Yes, the wife-murderer, once again.'

'Oh no, really? But I thought you'd told him I wouldn't be here until after eight?'

'Unfortunately, he went shopping in Storhampton this

afternoon and bumped into Elsa, who was tactless enough to mention that you'd been to lunch with her.'

'What a nuisance! But at least it doesn't appear to have struck him that I might be avoiding him deliberately. Or, if it has, he's ignoring it. Probably the second, I should say. He's too self-confident to allow snubs to deflect him from getting what he wants.'

'A necessary characteristic for the successful murderer, you might say?'

'Shouldn't wonder. I'm sure that's how Louise sees him, though, and I'd love her to be proved wrong. All the same, it might be a mistake to go there on my own. On the other hand, I'm rather keen to find out why he's so anxious that I should and also whether there have been any repercussions over the letter.'

'Well, I'm not offering to come with you, if that was in your mind.'

'No, I don't expect miracles, but you have given me an idea, Toby. Why don't I compromise and invite him here instead? You wouldn't mind that, would you?'

'Yes, I would. I can think of few things I should mind more.'

'Oh, you needn't appear. In fact, I should prefer you not to, but I shall lay heavy stress on the fact that you are upstairs hard at work, although not so hard that you wouldn't notice a scream or two from below. That should be protection enough, don't you think?'

'Not if he has caught up with my well-known reputation for cowardice. It might be safer to harp on Mrs Parkes' presence in the kitchen.'

'Yes, that's brilliant. I'll go and ring him up right away and say my car's broken down, or something or other and that, if he wants to see me, he must come and do it here.'

'Well, that was another non-starter,' I announced a few minutes later.

'So he won't come? What a shame! All our trouble for

44

nothing! Did you gain the impression that he considered it would be more prudent to murder you on home territory?'

'On the contrary, he said he'd be delighted, but unfortunately he'd invited some other people as well. Can you beat it? All that scheming and subterfuge and it turns out to be a perfectly normal social occasion.'

'Did he name the other guests?'

'Only Elsa. I must say she didn't say a word about it to me, but presumably he invited her when they met in Storhampton this afternoon.'

'So what will you do now?'

'Oh, I've said I'll go. I felt it was the least I could do, to make amends for my nasty suspicions. I told him I'd borrow your car. You don't mind, do you?'

'Not at all, but don't go leaping too far in the other direction. If you take my advice, you'll arrive late and then, if there are no other cars there, turn round and drive straight home again.'

'Yes,' I agreed. 'As someone recently remarked, it's a sad thing to be cursed with a suspicious mind, but the same precaution had already occurred to me.'

EIGHT

There were two cars on the grass border beside the white picket fence, although neither belonged to Elsa. One was a Range Rover, which had been there on my first visit, the other a pale blue estate car, which also looked familiar, although it was an unexpected place to find it.

Clearly, however, there was no need to retreat and I walked up the brick path, pushed open the front door, which was off the latch, and went inside.

In addition to our host, there were three people in the room. Elsa and Louise were sitting close together on one side and Tim, by himself, on the other. They were all looking with mesmerised expressions at James McGrath, who had taken up a commanding position, with his back to the fireplace, literally holding the floor with a dissertation on what, from the sentence or two I caught of it before he noticed me, sounded like ways and means of computer rigging.

Breaking off, he said: 'Ah, come in, come in! So glad you could make it. I was beginning to be afraid there'd been more car trouble.'

'No, sorry to be late, but I always drive like a snail in other people's property. Hallo, Elsa! And Tim and Louise! What a nice surprise!'

Neither of the Macadams responded to this with more than a nod, but Elsa plunged into a long-winded explanation about her last-minute invitation and how she had left her car at the Macadams, so that they could all come together.

While this was going on, our host was barging about the room, replenishing glasses, whether they needed it or not, and pulling up a chair for me, so that we were now grouped in a semi-circle facing the fireplace. He then resumed his

46

former position and announced:

'I'm glad you've come, Tessa, because what I have to say concerns you as well.'

No one spoke, but the two women shifted slightly in their chairs and Tim covered the lower half of his face with a handkerchief, presumably to conceal the nervous spasms which always betrayed him in moments of stress.

'Well, go on!' I said, breaking the silence and James obeyed.

'At about this time yesterday evening I had a visitor. His name was Superintendent Mackenzie and he had brought a document for my inspection. I expect you can guess what it was?'

Again no one answered and, turning now to Elsa and Louise, he said:

'I was given to understand that you had both seen it already, so I do not propose to waste time by telling you to whom it was addressed and what it consisted of.'

'You mean he told you?' Louise burst out. 'But . . . it was confidential . . . he promised . . .'

'No, Madam, he did not tell me who had given it to him, and nor do I intend to reveal how I came by the information.'

He had no need to, of course and, judging by her venomous look, Louise's feelings towards me had previously been as those of a mother for her ewe lamb, compared to what they had now sunk to. Elsa must have noticed it too, for she said:

'It was my fault, Louise. I'll explain it to you some time, but just now there are more important matters to discuss. Please go on, James!'

'Mackenzie asked me whether I recognised the handwriting and I said that, without being certain about it, it looked remarkably like my wife's. That wouldn't do for him. He wanted a straight yes or no, so I put on my reading glasses and did my best to advise him, but the curious thing was that I still couldn't be positive. On the whole, I was now inclined to believe that it was not Rosamund's writing. As some of

47

you know, she uses an italic script and, although there is a sameness between one person's and another's, there was something uncharacteristic about this one, although I was unable to define it.'

'Didn't he want to see something of hers to compare it with?' Elsa asked.

'Indeed, he did, Madam, and a very simple and obvious request it seemed. Surprisingly difficult to put into practice, however. She had taken her diary, address book and suchlike with her and I have never kept any of her letters to me, not even the most recent one. After a longish search, the best I could produce was a three line message on the telephone pad and an old shopping list in the kitchen drawer. It was enough, though.'

He paused here and looked round the room at each of us in turn, before repeating: 'It was enough.'

'Enough for what?' Louise asked.

'To tell us both that those two scraps had not been written by the same hand as the letter. Of the two of us, I should say that I was the more taken aback, which probably only shows me to be a less observant man than I had prided myself on being.'

Not resisting the temptation to show off, which is one of the saddening effects Louise has on me, I said:

'The explanation is more likely to be that the Superintendent, unlike you, was prepared for the letter to be a fake.'

'Evidently he was, but why?'

'Presumably because it had been through a fingerprint test, in which only two sets had been found, and both accounted for. Not many people write letters with gloves on.'

'Yes, I see what you mean. And so there you have it! As interested parties, or at any rate those with the most right to feel interested, I thought you should know how matters stand, although that was not my sole purpose in inviting you here this evening. I am now going to ask Louise and Elsa for their help.'

'I can't imagine what either of us could do,' Louise told

him in her most truculent voice.

'No, I daresay not, so I shall tell you. So far as I can see, the only way to bring this miserable business to anything approaching a satisfactory conclusion is to find out where Rosamund is, with the least possible delay. I, therefore, earnestly entreat you both to do all in your power to bring that about. Perhaps, if you were to put your heads together and fill some gaps in each other's knowledge, there might be a chance of our hitting on something to give us a lead.'

'I shall do my best,' Elsa assured him. 'We both will, but I'm afraid I can't offer you much encouragement. We have all been racking our brains over it for days and we are still just as much in the dark. And now, if that is all you have to tell us, I suppose we should be on our way.'

'But is it all?' Tim asked, speaking for the first time. 'I do find that hard to believe, if you'll excuse my saying so. Are we really to understand that the Superintendent left it there? Went away, with no more questions?'

'Indeed, you are not, sir. The part of the interview which I have just described was only the beginning. It lasted, in fact, for almost two hours, but since the rest of what passed between us seemed to concern no one but myself, I had not intended to repeat it. However, I have now changed my mind.'

'Which of us has done that for you?' I asked him.

'You have. Something tells me that when your friends get up to leave you will insist on leaving with them and, after what you have now heard, who should blame you? However, since you have shown yourself to be somewhat better informed than the rest of us, there is one point in particular on which I should value your opinion. May I tell you?'

'Of course you may.'

'There was an incident which occurred immediately after we had finished comparing the two sets of handwriting. The Superintendent asked me to read the letter and say whether I believed the statements it contained to be true. I replied that I did, for the simple reason that it was almost identical to a letter she had written to me before she went away. It was regrettable, to put it mildly, that I had destroyed it, but I had no difficulty in recalling every word. He then played what I regard as a neat trick. That being the case, he said, would I write it down for him? Now the question is this: am I right in assuming that this was a device to get me to put down in my own hand what amounted to a copy of the forged letter, so that experts might decide whether they were, or could have been written by the same person?'

'Yes, you are.'

'So here is one more for you to answer, if you will. Would it also be correct to assume that such a decision could not be regarded as conclusive, one way or the other? That, whatever the verdict, an element of doubt would remain? In short, that some other expert might be found whose opinion contradicted the first?'

'Not entirely. I think that would only apply if the result was positive. That's to say, if the first expert had given it as his opinion that they were written by the same person. In that case, I should imagine it would need to be endorsed by others before it could be accepted as proof. But, if he were to express doubts, or decide that it could not have been written by the same person, then that would most likely be the end of it, because it could not be used as evidence.'

'So I have nothing to fear? No, don't answer that. How could you and why should you? I realise how black things must look for me, but I do assure you that, if I were guilty, I should not now be wasting my time and yours by putting these questions. The matter would already be in the hands of my solicitor. So thank you all for coming and remember, if you will, what I have asked you to do for me.'

We drove in slow procession to the Macadam's house, Tim and Louise in their own car, Elsa and I followed in Toby's. This splitting into pairs had been done at the instigation of Louise, who was no doubt eager to hear my views, without putting herself to the trouble of asking for them. Responding to this unspoken command, Elsa had scarcely climbed aboard before saying:

'Well, what do you make of it, Tessa? How can one possibly believe that anyone but he forged the letter? And yet, at the same time, he sounded so convincing, specially with that bit at the end.'

'I don't know, Elsa. Like you, I'm in two minds about it, but it struck me as rational, as well as convincing. Why should he bother to consult an amateur like myself, if he had forged it and therefore knew that not one, but a dozen experts could be found to say so?'

'So you're inclined to take him on trust?'

'Yes, I am. The alternative would appear to be that he's exceptionally stupid, which is much harder to believe. There are a couple of things I'd need to find out though, before finally coming down on his side. Perhaps you could take on one of them for me?'

'I suppose it depends on what it is.'

'I'd be interested to know whether Rosamund could type. If so, whether she owned a typewriter. That would really clinch it for me.'

'Yes, I see what you mean. At least, I think I do.'

'You see, I can understand what the purpose of sending a spurious letter to Louise would have been. To allay her suspicions and ensure that the news that Rosamund had bolted would come from the most reliable source of all. But what a fearful risk to have tried to imitate her handwriting for such an insignificant reward! To lie low and do nothing would have been far more sensible. Louise could hardly have gone to the police to complain that she hadn't heard from her friend lately and therefore concluded that her husband had murdered her. If Rosamund did possess a portable typewriter, which she could have taken with her, all he needed to do, presuming he killed her, was to type the letter, sign it with a big R, then sink the machine in the river Thames.'

'Well, I expect it would be quite easy to find out. Louise is bound to know.'

'Bound to,' I agreed.

'What's the other job?'

'Oh, that's for Robin. I must remember to ask him when he comes for the weekend.'

'But surely you can tell me what it is?'

'In the event of the letter being proved to have been written by James, I want to know what will happen next. Presumably, they can't arrest him for murder until a body turns up, so will they send seven men with seven spades to Orchard House, to start looking for one? Whichever way they tackle it, I see boulders ahead and it's made more complicated still by the fact that no one seems clear about exactly when Rosamund is supposed to have walked out. You said that Tim and Louise had been away for the weekend and when they'd got back she'd gone, but that's pretty vague and no one seems able to pin it down any closer. I shall be fascinated to know what the procedure is likely to be now.'

'If you had arrived back five minutes earlier,' Toby said, 'You would have had the unique opportunity to answer one of your own telephone calls.'

'Oh, sorry, I'm afraid I dawdled a bit. Who was it this time?'

'The usual. If you ask me, he fancies you. That's the simple answer and all this intrigue about his missing wife has been cooked up as a cheap way to gain your sympathy.'

'Then he must feel cheated because it is turning out to be a most expensive way. What does he want now?'

'The same as he always wants. He would like you to have dinner with him tomorrow evening.'

'Nothing doing. I'm working tomorrow and, even if I weren't, I wouldn't have dinner with him.'

'You may change you mind when you've heard it all.'

'All right, tell me.'

'He is too canny to invite you to dine with him in the privacy of his lair and he suggests that you should meet him in the foyer of that hotel whose name temporarily escapes me, but as far as I know is the only one in Oxford.'

'Oh, I see!'

'He also went out of his way to emphasise that he will be unable to drive you home afterwards. This, of course, is to allay any fears you might have of finishing up as a mangled corpse on the hard shoulder of the M40.'

'Did he say so?'

'Not in those words. His explanation was that after dinner he has to drive to some place in Northampton, where he has business to conduct tomorrow in his role of Capability Brown.'

'Well, if I go at all, it will have to be for a quick drink. I can't expect the studio driver to hang around for the whole evening.'

'So now you think you will go?'

'I shall weigh up the pros and cons while I have a bath. That usually brings a decision, for better or worse.'

NINE

'The architects of this building went to immense trouble to ensure that the acoustics should be as bad as human ingenuity could make them,' he said, steering me to a corner table, 'which of course is why I chose it. I should prefer what I have to say to be heard by no one but yourself.'

'Whatever it is, I hope you'll be able to compress it into half an hour. The car is coming for me at seven thirty.'

'I shall do my best and perhaps I ought to begin by saying that, whatever appearances may suggest, I did not forge the letter and I did not kill Rosamund. I don't know whether you feel able to take that on trust, but I hope so, because if not, you will certainly not believe anything else I am about to tell you.'

'For the sake of argument, let us assume that I do.'

'Thank you for that much, at any rate. And the next point to get out of the way is that I do not know who committed either of those crimes, but I have now decided that I must make it my business to find out.'

'Hang on a moment, James, because I must interrupt you here. Are you now implying that you know your wife is dead?'

'I have known it from the beginning,' he replied.

'And that note you told Louise she had left for you, saying that she had gone off with another man?'

'Never existed. Or rather, it had an existence once upon a time, but that was several years ago.'

'And yet you still expect me to believe . . . ?'

'I know it sounds unreasonable, but if you will let me explain, I hope to make you understand. It is the brunt of what I have to tell you and, since you are in a hurry, it might be best if I were to present the facts in my own way and in the right order.'

'Oh, very well.'

'To return to the point I was making before, it is not hard to see that, due to a combination of circumstances, for which I am partly to blame, I am getting into very deep water and it is now my considered opinion that the only way to extricate myself is by discovering the true perpetrator of these crimes. And please don't try to persuade me that I should leave such business to the police, because it would only waste more time. The single advantage I possess is that they may be halted in their tracks by lack of evidence. To make them a free gift of it and to expect them to take it for what it was, and not for what they could make it, would be the sheerest lunacy. If you, who are on the whole predisposed in my favour, have reservations, I can guess what their reaction would be.'

'And what gives you the idea that I am predisposed in your favour?'

'The fact that you have twice eaten my salt, or drunk my gin and tonic, to be precise. I believe you to possess integrity, as well as brains. I do not see you accepting hospitality from someone you thought capable of killing a defenceless woman.'

No sweeter sound on earth, as a rule, than a song in one's own praise, but this one contained a few wrong notes as well.

'And some fine old whoppers you told me while I was drinking it,' I reminded him.

'Yes, and I apologise, but you caught me off guard. Naturally, I knew the letter must be a forgery, but the rest of what I told you was substantially true. I honestly did feel a sense of relief. It seemed to me that it could only have been written by Rosamund's murderer and this, after the first shock, struck me as a good sign. He had expected me to be under arrest and awaiting trial by now, but the weeks had gone by and I was still at large. So he was getting panicky and had decided to give matters a push forward by sending this letter, counting on its being recognised as a fake. For a time I even allowed myself to believe that, now that it was in the hands of the police, they would be able to track down the author and reveal him as the murderer as well. It wasn't until later that I realised what a forlorn hope that was.'

'I don't necessarily agree with you there, but there isn't time to argue about it now. That is, if there is more to come?'

'Indeed there is, and I now turn to some events which occurred one Saturday morning last April. I should warn you that it is not a pretty story.'

'Stories about murder rarely are.'

'I take a keen interest in bird watching, as you know, and on the morning in question, as on numerous others at this time of year, I got up between three and four o'clock and went on foot to one of my favourite look-outs. It happens to be high up in the woods which adjoin our land, and I have rigged up a rough sort of hide. Our house is very isolated, as you also know, and the sun wasn't up when I set out. The Macadams were away and, not surprisingly, I didn't encounter a soul, either then or on my way back about three hours later. In fact, I was home just after eight o'clock. Everything was the same as I had left it. The empty milk bottles were still outside the back door and neither the post nor the papers had been delivered. Nothing surprising there, either. Situated as we are, at the furthest point from the village, our deliveries don't arrive before nine-thirty or ten. I put the kettle on to make some tea and then carried a tray upstairs for Rosamund. There wasn't a sound and the door was shut, so I opened it very gently, in case she was still asleep. I needn't have bothered. She wouldn't have heard, if it had been forced open by a herd of elephants.'

'She was dead?'

'Such an idea never entered my head at the time. I did notice that the bed was rumpled and untidy, because it was so out of character. She was always neat and meticulous. But still, I just assumed that she'd got up earlier than usual and had gone into the bathroom.'

'But she wasn't there?'

'No, nor anywhere else in the house. Early morning walks weren't her style at all, so I was left with only one conclusion.'

'That she'd walked out?'

'I knew I shouldn't have to waste time explaining things to you, Tessa. Before I'd finished drinking my tea, I'd become half convinced of it. She had known I would be out between four and eight in the morning and she'd ordered a taxi to take her to Dedley Station in time for the first train of the day. Then I realised that there was a simple way to find out for certain. If she had left me, she must have taken a suitcase with her and the contents must have included, among other things, brushes and combs and make-up. The answer was to find out what, if anything, was missing from her dressing-table.'

'And now I suppose you're going to tell me that everything was present and correct?'

'I feel sure it was, but I never got as far as looking. In order to reach the dressing-table, I had to pass the bed and, in doing so, I made a series of discoveries, each one acting like an electric shock to the brain and nerves.'

'What discoveries?'

'Bloodstains on the pillow was the first one. Also on the mattress cover.'

'Mattress cover?'

'The bottom sheet had been removed. That was my second discovery. The third was the knife. It had been tucked down under the pile of rumpled bedclothes, with only an inch or two of the handle showing.'

'Did you touch it?'

'No, I pulled back the bedclothes until the whole length of it was visible. The blade and lower half of the handle were caked with blood.'

'What kind of a knife was it?'

'A familiar one. My own pet carving knife, in fact. Used only by myself and always kept sharp as a razor. I pride myself on my skill as a carver, you see. It is one of my vanities, and not the first one to get me into trouble.'

'Then what?'

'I stood there like a zombie for I can't say how long, incapable of thought or movement. By the time I'd pulled myself together and gone downstairs the tea was cold, so I made a fresh pot. What I wanted more than anything was a neat whisky, but I didn't dare have it because I needed a clear head to try and work out what I was going to do.'

'I don't understand. Why was it necessary to do anything, except go to the telephone and ring the police?'

'A good question, for which there are three good answers. In the first place, there was nothing and nobody, as I've explained, to bear out my story of the bird-watching expedition. It is a well-known hobby of mine and one which is obviously known to my wife's murderer, but there was no way of proving that I had indulged in it on that particular morning. It is not like shooting, where, with any luck, you have something to show for it. That was the first reason.'

'What else?'

'Something which occurred in my raffish youth. I was plastered and I got mixed up in a pub brawl. It was a genuine case of self-defence, or so I believed. This chap came at me and I let him have it. I was a good bit younger and stronger than he was and he went down like a sack of potatoes. He died in hospital about eight hours later and I was up on a manslaughter charge. I got off, as it happens, but it was touch and go, and it's still there in the records. A reputation for violence wasn't going to be much help in these circumstances.'

'And the third reason?'

'That took care of the motive. Good old fashioned jealousy, which is a beauty, isn't it? You remember my telling you that the letter Rosamund was supposed to have left for me had once existed? Well, it had. A year or two ago she really did go off with another man. I was away on a job in Hereford and I came back to find her gone and this note on her dressing-table. It made a deep impression on me and when Louise came round, bleating about Rosamund not being with her cousin and I had to switch stories, I was word perfect.'

'But she came back to you that time?'

'Yes. I never quite understood why, but she came back and we tried to pick things up where we'd left off, but she wasn't happy. I think she was still seeing this man, corresponding with him, anyway. That was partly why we moved to Sowerley. I thought a change of scene and new friends might help her to forget him. They didn't though, and it would all have come out, if I'd been put on trial, because I'm pretty sure her cousin must have known about it.'

'So when you had drunk your tea, what did you do?'

'I started by packing two suitcases, the smaller one with the kind of things a woman would need if she were going away for a few days, the other with the knife and bloodstained bedclothes. I left them in the bedroom, let myself out of the house, locked the front and back doors, got in the car and drove to Banbury. Luckily, I wasn't expecting anyone that day and the post and newspapers had both been delivered by then.'

'Why Banbury, for God's sake?'

'I had an appointment there with a client at eleven o'clock and it was important not to deviate from the day's programme. My meeting was to include lunch and I reckoned that I should be back at home between four-thirty and five, although I'd have been happy to have spun it out longer than that, if the circumstances had made it seem natural.'

'Why?'

'Because it would still have given me several more hours of daylight than I needed. When there was still just enough left to get to the main road without using headlights, I carried the suitcases down to the car and drove to the place I had planned for their disposal. It would not help you to know where that was.'

'And also you may not be willing to put yourself in my power quite to that extent?'

'No, perhaps not. Any other questions?'

'Dozens, but I only have time for two. Did you never find out who the man was who Rosamund ran off with?'

'No, but I intend to do everything in my power to do so now because it seems to me that he must be the one who murdered her. God knows why, but who else could it have been?'

'You mean because of the forged letter? I agree with you

that whoever sent it was most likely also the murderer, but why does it follow that no one but your wife's lover could have written it?'

'Because in saying that it was almost a facsimile of the one which Rosamund had written to me two years earlier, I was speaking the exact truth. It had been pored over often enough before I destroyed it, to have become indelibly imprinted on my memory, and who else but Rosamund, myself and her lover could have seen the original? No doubt, she would have shown it to him, conceivably have written it as he dictated, but it passes belief that it could have been read by anyone else. That was why I asked Louise and Elsa for their help. I thought it was just possible that one of them might come up with some memory, however trivial, which would give me a lead. What was your last question?'

'The obvious one. Why have you told me all this?'

'Because I need your help. I could see from the expression on Louise's face that my appeal had been useless. I have an idea that she knows more than she's told us, but I'm not the one to get it out of her. She's no friend to me.'

'Nor to me either.'

'That may be, but it's not true of Elsa, is it? She's the one I'd like you to work on. If Louise is concealing something, perhaps Elsa can find out what it is. As far as I can see, it's my only chance. Will you at least try?'

'I'll think about it,' I said, getting up. 'No promises, but I will think about it. And now I must go. My driver is the soul of punctuality.'

'I daresay there's not much point in my saying this,' he replied, also standing up, 'but despite all the white lies I've told in the past, this time I have been completely honest with you. I hope you believe that?'

'And I'll be completely honest with you,' I told him. 'Just now I'm not sure whether I do or not.'

TEN

Robin arrived on Friday and Elsa invited the three of us to dinner on Saturday evening. All the Laycock family were to be there, as well as Marc and Millie, Mrs Laycock having given it out that she was feeling better and would welcome a change of scene.

'And she must be better,' Elsa added, 'for Louise tells me that the nurse has now left.'

Toby flatly refused to go, declaring that he did not care for the sound of the Laycocks and that even a four-hour spell devoted exclusively to answering the telephone would be preferable to their company. Robin was not enthusiastic either, but I melted his resistance by warning him that he would give Elsa an inferiority complex if he persisted in wriggling out of all her invitations, for I could not bear to pass up this opportunity to meet the mysterious step-mother.

'In fact the opportunity became over-extended because things worked out in such a way that after dinner I was stuck with her for almost an hour. Before this, however, there had been a short but spirited altercation between Gregory Laycock and, of all people, Millie, mercifully not witnessed by Elsa, who was out in the kitchen making coffee.

The minute dinner was over Marc and Andrea drifted off somewhere on their own, and when the rest of us had assembled in the other room Gregory remained standing with his back to the fireplace, gazing expectantly at the door and taking no part in the conversation. He then informed us that he could not imagine what had become of Andrea.

'Marc has taken her to the pub,' Millie explained.

'Taken her where? I don't understand what you mean.'

'Pub. P.U.B.,' she said, getting it right, luckily. 'You know, short for public house. He is going to teach her to play

61

darts.'

'But this is outrageous! How dare he take my daughter into such a place, without permission? He must be stopped at once.'

'Too late for that. They left ten minutes ago, so they'll be there by now. And I don't suppose it occurred to my brother that he needed your permission.'

'Then he has a lot to learn, your brother, as he will shortly find out.'

'Oh, don't worry! It's a very nice pub and all the customers are frightfully well-behaved. Unlike some!' she added in a scornful undertone.

It was as well that the door was pushed open at this point and Elsa entered with the coffee tray. Making a visible effort to control himself, Gregory darted forward to take it from her and while she was pouring it out fell into earnest conversation with her about some historic building which the Storhampton Council was proposing to demolish, to make way for a new car park.

Millie, meanwhile, had trained her guns on Robin. She was a dear girl and had evidently got her macrobiotic diet under control, for she had fined down a lot during the past year. She still had much to learn about the social graces, however, and was submitting Robin to a lecture on unilateral disarmament, which she appeared to be in favour of. He was either too kindhearted to get up and walk away, or, more likely, feared that by doing so, he might be landed with Mrs Laycock, which would be worse still. If so, he had made the right decision, for she was a sad disappointment.

She had appeared to be unmoved by the absurd fracas which her husband had created, but I suspected that apathy had become a way of life for her. If this was one of her good days, I should have hated to see her on a bad one, and anyone less fitted for the role of wicked stepmother could never have existed. She was a putty-faced woman with colourless hair and a colourless personality to match, with only her large, sad brown eyes to indicate that she might once have been attractive. Now, she had evidently come to think so little of herself as to go out to dinner looking unkempt and none too clean and with two or three single hairs sprouting from her chin, which reminded me so forcibly of gooseberry tails that it was both disagreeable to look at them and hard to look away.

This rebarbative appearance and lack-lustre manner probably both owed something to the fact that she ate very little and drank nothing but soda water throughout the evening. She smoked incessantly, however, causing Millie, who holds uncompromising views on pollution, to be in danger of bursting every blood vessel she possessed.

Elsa, it seemed, had been correct in the matter of the arthritis, for Mrs Laycock was unable to walk without a stick and an arm to lean on, and then only with difficulty. All in all, it was hard to imagine her having the strength or will to kill a spider and any attempt of that sort might well have ended with her dying from fright of the spider.

We talked about the weather, we discussed some good books we had or had not read recently and we touched on the new car park. I asked her a number of questions about her house and garden and she reciprocated by asking me one or two about the television serial. I don't think she can have listened very carefully to the answers, though, because after a particularly heavy silence she began asking the same questions all over again.

However, as Elsa had recently had cause to remind me, people are seldom all of a piece and after we had lurched on to the subject of where I lived, some signs of animation began to appear:

'It would have to be London for us,' I had explained, 'whether we liked it or not, because of Robin's job.'

'Oh, but you must like it, don't you? I'd give anything to be back there myself.'

'You don't care for the country?'

'I loathe it,' she answered with unexpected vehemence and I noticed that Gregory, who was sitting nearby with

63

Elsa, looked up and shook his head at her.

'What made you come here, then?'

'Oh, it was Greg's idea. I think it was for Andrea's sake, mainly. She'd told him how much she enjoyed the holidays she'd spent here as a child and how she used to dread going back to London when they were over. Her life is one long holiday now.'

Not being sure how to respond to this, I let it drop and she then rocked me right back on my heels by saying:

'Tell me something: have you ever been in a fire?'

'Only a simulated one, I'm thankful to say.'

'Oh . . . what does that mean?'

'It was for a film, you see. Me, waking up in a smoke-filled room, cut to the exterior of the building, with flames leaping out of an upstairs window.'

'All the same, it must have been terrifying?'

'No, I'm sorry to disillusion you, but they'd shot the exteriors weeks before we got to the smoke-filled room and I was nowhere near.'

'Oh, I see! You must think me very simple.'

'No, why should you know about such tricks of the trade? But what made you ask? Is it a particular phobia of yours?'

'No, but last night I dreamt the house was on fire. It was horrible. So real and vivid that even when I woke up I imagined I could still smell burning. I don't know, though. Perhaps that was part of the dream and one shouldn't bore people with one's silly nightmares, I know that. I wonder if Greg's ready to leave yet? I'm feeling a little tired. I sleep very badly and I get so easily tired nowadays.'

'I'll go and tell him,' I said, bouncing up before she could change her mind.

'Arthritis?' Robin said in the car going home. 'Who said anything about arthritis?'

'Elsa did.'

'Oh, Elsa! Just because she goes through life with blinkers on is no reason why you should.'

'Well, I don't know why you say that, Robin. She's certainly very lame and not at all well either, I should have said.'

'Quite so, but it is not caused by arthritis.'

'What then?'

'Everything points to the fact that she either is, or has been a confirmed alcoholic.'

'Do you mean that?'

'It's not the kind of thing one says without meaning it.'

'No, and now I'm getting used to the idea, I wonder that I didn't see it for myself. She has all my sympathy too. Life with that horrible man and his odious spoilt daughter would be enough to drive anyone to drink. I wonder if Elsa has known about this all along and was just being discreet? There are a number of things I want to ask Elsa, when I get time, but perhaps I won't bother her with this one. It would only upset her and it is far too tame a story to be worth that.'

I might have added that it was also likely to be a story with no ending, but life can be just as unpredictable as people and, by a startling coincidence, only forty-eight hours later the Laycocks' house caught on fire.

The damage was not extensive, being confined to one small room on the ground floor, but by the time it was discovered Mrs Laycock had died from fumes and suffocation.

ELEVEN

The history of this sad event, as it filtered down to me through all the usual channels, was as follows:

Gregory Laycock had returned home later than usual on Monday evening, having attended a reception for some international medical conference. The invitation had been accepted weeks in advance, when there was a nurse on the premises, but he had not changed his mind about going, having received an undertaking from Andrea that she would spend the evening at home.

However, she had either, as she claimed, mistaken the date, or had become bored by her stepmother's company and at six o'clock had taken herself off to London, to dine and go to the cinema with Marc, not getting back until the early hours of Tuesday morning.

When Gregory had arrived home at about half past ten the house was in darkness and he had gone straight to the morning-room, which was situated at the back of the house and had now been turned into a bedroom for his wife. This was a hastily improvised arrangement, which had come into being when the nurse left and there was no longer someone always at hand to help her up and down stairs.

There had been no need to open the door to ascertain that she was asleep, because her snores had been audible from three feet away and, without pausing to question whether there might be something abnormal about their pitch and volume, he turned away, went to his own room and fell asleep until Andrea woke him up again.

He had not heard her come in, but had first been aroused by the sound of slamming doors and running taps. After that, when all was quiet once more, he had found difficulty in going back to sleep and had spent the next two or three hours slipping in and out of dozes, each bringing its own, or a continuation of its predecessor's dream. The last of these, although he was unaware of it, was a replica of one his wife had had only two days earlier and when it was over and he was wide awake once more, the impression remained that the house was on fire.

For a while he tried to ignore it and to persuade himself that it was his imagination, but then he remembered that Andrea was fully capable of leaving a lighted cigarette in the drawing-room, or one of the burners switched on in the kitchen and he had forced himself to go downstairs and investigate.

Smoke was wafting out from under the morning-room door and when he flung it open the atmosphere inside was so dense that all he could see was that the draught he had now created had injected an extra spurt of energy into the flames which had already got a hold on one of the curtains.

He had managed to take a few steps in the direction of the newly installed bed, but was then overpowered by smoke and fumes and had been forced to retreat into the hall. Gasping for breath, he had closed the door behind him and then telephoned the Fire Brigade, before going upstairs to wake Andrea. As he later discovered, if he had succeeded in penetrating a yard or two further inside the room, he might have stumbled over the recumbent figure of his wife. She was found lying face down on the floor, one arm outstretched and the walking stick at her side, midway between the bed and the door. Although it was estimated that the fire had been going for between two and three hours, there was a bare possibility that when he came on the scene she was still alive.

Two other discoveries which the room yielded were an empty gin bottle and an ashtray overflowing with half-smoked cigarettes and spent matches.

Naturally, it was several days before the full story came out and I did not even hear the beginning of it until I got back from work on Tuesday evening. It did not have so much impact as might have been expected, my mind by then being beset by problems far removed from the remorseless extermination of the female population of Sowerley.

This was due to my agent having come on a visit to the location, ostensibly for the routine business of casting a professional eye over the precedings, but in reality, as I discovered over lunch, to press her case for the television serial. In doing so, she had dangled enough golden carrots in front of my nose to tempt a far less acquisitive spirit than mine.

'But you were the one who pointed out that sixteen weeks in L.A. might not do much for my marriage,' I reminded her.

'I know that, my dearest, and no one wants to upset darling old Robin, least of all me, but I have not been idle, you know. I've really been working very hard for you, and I think you'll agree that it's good news.'

'What is?'

'I've talked them into allowing you a clause in your contract, giving you a two-week break in the middle for a lovely little hols. You can fly home at their expense. There now, isn't that something?'

It was certainly something which needed as much digesting, in its own way, as the roast pork, potatoes, cabbage, apple sauce and stuffing, and avarice and better judgement were still fighting it out when I arrived back at Roakes at half past eight.

Toby was in the dining-room, chumping away at something which looked suspiciously like roast pork.

'Yours is drying out on what, in the pre-Florida era, was known as the hot plate,' he informed me, 'and is now called the cuisinette.'

'I don't think I'll bother, not very hungry. Rather late for your dinner, isn't it?'

'Yes, far too late and all the fault of that tiresome Elsa, who dropped in, as she put it, on her way home from Dedley. I can only say that she must have been lost in a reverie and in no state to drive at all, since it can't have taken her less than eight miles out of her way.'

'Could she remember why she'd dropped in?'

'I suppose she was hoping to see you and be first with the news. It was a great bore because she would neither go away, nor stay for dinner. I think you are wise not to have any, it is badly overcooked.'

'First with what news?'

'Be so good as to fetch the strawberries,' he replied, 'and you shall hear.'

'I wish now that she had waited to tell you herself. Judging by your wooden expression, I have not succeeded in wringing the last drop of drama from it.'

'There's not much drama to be wrung, is there? Just rather squalid and sad. Only two points of minor interest that I can see.'

'Better than nothing. What are they?'

'Well, it's curious that she should have had a premonition about it, don't you think? On the other hand, I suppose it could easily be explained by assuming that this wasn't the first time she'd dropped a lighted cigarette on the bedclothes and what she experienced wasn't a dream, but the real smell of scorching.'

'So, after all, it's not even of minor interest?'

'Something I find more arresting is that, if she was an alcoholic, and it looks as though Robin was right about that, why did they allow her to get her hands on the gin bottle?'

'Yes, Elsa was puzzled too.'

'So she did know? The arthritis was just a whitewash?'

'It seems that Louise had tipped her off. In the strictest confidence, I need hardly say.'

'Oh, that Louise! She crops up everywhere, doesn't she? And how does Louise account for Mrs Laycock hobbling off to bed, with a bottle of gin tucked underneath her arm?'

'She is unable to account for it. All the booze in that house is kept under lock and key and Gregory never leaves the house without the key in his pocket.'

'Oh, well, I suppose the poor creature bribed someone to

get hold of a bottle for her. Or maybe just rang up her husband's wine merchant and asked them to deliver one. That would be the simple answer.'

'A sight too simple, perhaps. One can hardly conceive that they wouldn't have been warned.'

'So we shall have to wait for the inquest and see what that brings forth. When is it, by the way?'

'I have no idea. You'll have to ask Louise.'

'Well, all I hope is that it doesn't occur to anyone to call Andrea as a witness. It is a chance I can't see her failing to make the most of.'

'Oh, these coroners are very experienced and know how to shut people up when they get carried away. No doubt he would pin her down to a couple of questions and send her packing, before she could get into her stride.'

'Which couple of questions, Toby?'

'Oh, I don't know. What time she got home and whether she happened to notice that the house was on fire, are two which spring to mind. And I would be interested to know why you are staring at me like that?'

'I am staring at you like this because you have just put into words a thought which has been hovering in the background for the past ten minutes. I was wrong when I said there were two curious features about this incident. There are three and the third and most puzzling hinges on Andrea. It is a question of time sequence, you see. I am prepared to believe that when Gregory arrived home his wife had only just fallen asleep and therefore the burning cigarette had barely started its devilish work. In other words, no conflagration, just a faint smell of scorching, too faint to be detected by anyone outside the room. You agree?'

'I see what you mean.'

'Of course you do; the story goes that Andrea didn't come home until two hours later and it is hard to believe that things would have stayed dormant during all this time. Surely, the fire would have got a hold by then and she would have noticed it as soon as she opened the front door?'

'I see what you mean, but it doesn't follow that I agree with you. There could be several reasons why she didn't.'

'Name a few!'

'One is that Mrs Laycock woke up again at some point after the other two had gone to bed and decided to treat herself to another cigarette.'

'I don't think much of that. In fact, I regard it as highly unlikely.'

'Well, try this one. The fact that Andrea didn't start crashing about in the bathroom until her father had been asleep for a couple of hours doesn't necessarily mean that she'd only just come in. She could have spent the time quietly in her bedroom, doing her nails or her yoga, or writing up her diary, for all we know.'

'Well yes, I suppose I have to admit that's conceivable, but I still consider that a hell of a long time went by without either of them noticing anything wrong.'

'Implying that one or both of them did notice that the room was on fire, but decided there was nothing to be done about it until the morning?'

'Quite so.'

'Then you must be slipping.'

'Why is that?'

'On a good day you'd have had one or both of them planting the bottle of gin beside her bed, waiting for it to take effect and then tossing some lighted cigarettes around.'

'Well, now that you mention it . . .'

'So it had crossed your mind?'

'No, but it's crossing it now and it wouldn't surprise me at all if you'd hit on the answer. Andrea is definitely loony and her Daddy strikes me as completely ruthless. As far as I can see, it's just a toss-up as to which one of them did it.'

'It will be interesting to see whether the Coroner and jury agree with you.'

'Even money they won't, but one can never be sure of anything these days. I think I'll go and find something to eat, after all. Solving mysteries always works up an appetite.'

TWELVE

Elsa had had a letter, which she handed to me when I called on her the following afternoon, shooting having been abandoned for the day, owing to bad weather and a worse forecast.

'Who's Isobel Ferguson?' I asked, looking at the signature first.

'Read it and you'll see. Read it aloud, in fact,' she said and I did so:

Dear Mrs Carrington,

Please forgive me for writing to you out of the blue like this, but I have been growing increasingly worried about my cousin Rosamund ever since my chance meeting with Louise Macadam in London a few weeks ago. She was under the impression that Rosamund was staying with me, but in fact I had not seen or heard from her for some time, and nor have I seen her since.

There was something particularly disturbing about the account Mrs Macadam gave me of Rosamund's reason for having come to London and that evening I made the first of several attempts to ring her myself. Throughout the first forty-eight hours I could get no reply at all, so concluded that Mrs Macadam had got hold of the wrong end of the stick and that my cousin and her husband were away somewhere together. But I still couldn't quite get it out of my mind, so a day or two later I tried again and this time James answered. When I asked if I could speak to Rosamund he at first tried to fob me off, saying that she had gone to stay with some friends in Sussex. I wasn't satisfied and I asked him to let me have their telephone number, as I had something urgent to discuss with her. He finally admitted that she had left him for another man and that he had no idea where she had gone or how to get in touch with her.

He then asked me to keep this to himself, as he was positive that she would come back and he thought they stood a better chance of patching things up and starting afresh, if the gossips and scandalmongers could be kept at bay.

It was a shock, of course, but not a shattering one, because I have to confess that I have never liked James and often wondered how she had managed to put up with him for so long. What did upset me was that she had not given me so much as a hint of what she planned to do. It was like a slap in the face, but I still felt certain that I should be hearing from her as soon as she felt secure that the break had truly been made and she could begin to settle down in her new life.

It was only when the weeks continued to drag by, with still no word from her, that it began to occur to me that James might have been lying, that there was some other explanation for her silence and that it was up to me to find out what it was.

You will be wondering, I am sure, that I should presume on our very brief acquaintance to burden you with my family problems. but I have heard Rosamund speak of you with affection and it seemed to me that you were one of the few congenial people she had found on her new surroundings. I felt I owed it to you to let you know that I have now taken the very grave step of applying to the police for help in tracing her. They did not, as I had feared, ridicule my suggestion that there could be some sinister reason for her disappearance and the only thing I regret is that is must inevitably involve you and other of her friends in a certain amount of unpleasantness. I hope you can forgive me for this and understand my feeling that the time had come for some action to be taken.

I want you to know that I have not done so without the approval of Alan, my husband, who fully supports me in this.

Yours sincerely,
Isobel Ferguson.

'Well, well!', I said, putting the letter down, 'There's a coincidence for you!'

'You mean that she should also have reported it to the police?'

'No, not that. In fact, I wonder she waited so long.'

'What I found surprising,' Elsa said, 'and disappointing, I must confess, is how much less straightforward Rosamund was than the woman we took her for. All that pretence about she and Isobel being so devoted that they hardly let a week go by without seeing each other! Louise and I were completely taken in and all the time it wasn't her cousin she had gone to see at all, but this lover of hers.'

'By the way, has Louise seen this letter?'

'No, and I haven't decided yet whether to show it to her or not. On the whole I feel inclined not to.'

'Why's that? I thought you and she were acting as a team in this affair?'

'Well, you see, Tessa, the letter doesn't actually tell us any more than we knew already, does it? And when I told you I was disappointed to discover how she had fooled us, it is nothing to what Louise's reaction would be. She prides herself on being perceptive about people and she'd feel humiliated, as well as angry. Also . . . well, of couse, I wouldn't say this to anyone but you, but the fact is, you know, that Louise can be a little touchy sometimes.'

'I do know, Elsa, none better.'

'And what inclines me most of all not to show her the letter is knowing how cross she would be that it was written to me and not her. And there, I consider, she would be justified. After all, she was the first to befriend Rosamund and she saw much more of her than I ever did. If it's true that Rosamund spoke of me to her cousin, then she must have spoken far more often of Louise and I find it inexplicable that I should have been singled out in this way.'

'I don't, but I won't tell you why because compliments embarrass you. I accept your other arguments, though, and I think they make sense, but do let me tell you about that coincidence. It came right at the end, when she mentioned her husband. Isobel Ferguson meant nothing to me, but Alan Ferguson is a different cup of tea.'

'Don't tell me you know him?'

'Not well, but Robin does. He's had a lot of dealings with one Alan Ferguson over the years.'

'Why? Is he a criminal?'

'Quite the reverse, they're on the same side. He works for an insurance group, what they call an assessor.'

'One of those people who sniff out the fraudulent claims?'

'Arson, in particular. In which field our Alan Ferguson happens to be one of the world's experts. That's why so many of his investigations end up in the lap of Scotland Yard. I wonder if it could be the same one? Can you remember what he looked like?'

'I only met them once and that was some time ago, but I should say he was about forty-five. Not good looking, but not unattractive either, as far as I remember.'

'Yes, that description fits.'

'It would fit a thousand men and it's not such an uncommon name.'

'No, but our Alan also lives in London and has a wife.'

'All the same, Tessa, if he should turn out to be Robin's friend, I still can't see how it would help us to discover what has become of Rosamund.'

'Ah well, in this case, you can't afford to overlook anything, however trivial. I think I'll get Robin to bring him home for a drink one evening. He's done it once to twice before, so there wouldn't be anything unnatural about it. I'll make a point of being there when he comes and then perhaps we'll at least find out something about Rosamund from the point of view of a not unattractive, middle-aged, exceptionally observant cousin-by-marriage.'

THIRTEEN

No investigation of the kind in which Alan Ferguson specialised was called for in the case of the Laycocks' fire. The damage was considered to be too negligible to be worth claiming for and at the inquest the jury brought in a verdict of Death by Misadventure.

The Coroner, evidently a non-smoker, had some strictures to make about the reckless folly of smoking in bed, but no reference was made to the empty gin bottle, so he either did not know of its existence, or else regarded drinking in bed as acceptable.

The report on these proceedings came from Millie Carrington, who had taken the day off from her secretarial college in order to observe them from the public gallery. This was no idle truancy, but had been undertaken for the laudable purpose of gaining experience for her career in journalism. It was a bit of luck for me, too, because it had inspired her to take down every word in shorthand, most of which, with the aid of memory, she was later able to transcribe. Although the spelling was on the eccentric side, the Coroner, for instance, being sometimes referred to as the Corner and sometimes as the Coronorer, it was possible to follow the gist.

Evidently, Millie was also unaware of the gin bottle's existence, for she did not comment on its omission from the evidence and I did not consider it my job to enlighten her.

'Well, come on!' she said the moment I had finished reading. 'Tell me what you think. You can give me your honest opinion. I shan't mind a bit if you say it's terrible.'

Taking 'honest opinion' to be euphemism for 'steady stream of unqualified praise', I said:

'Not terrible at all. It's first rate and I'm most impressed.

Only one tiny comment.'

'What's that?'

'Well, you see, Millie, if you'd been writing it for *The Times* or one of those, I'd say you'd hit exactly the right note, but some of the popular papers might find it a little too dry and factual. Their readers look for a human touch here and there. It might be an idea to start off with something about tragedy hitting the bustling little market town of Storhampton. All deaths are tragic, you know, and all little market towns are expected to bustle. And how about Andrea? Surely, she was able to introduce a dash of the histrionics? What was she wearing, for instance?'

'Black, wouldn't you know?'

'It might be worth mentioning that when you do the re-write. You could even have her with bowed head, brushing away a tear.'

'There weren't any tears to brush.'

'That's beside the point. Still, you're the pro and you must do as you think best. What was she like when she gave her evidence?'

'Pretty hopeless, really. She started off at a gallop, all that rot about how she'd risked her life by going into the room after her father came out, to try and rescue her stepmother, but the Coroner squashed her completely by asking her to speak up, please, because he couldn't hear a word she was saying.'

'Not choked with emotion, by any chance?'

'No, but I think she was nervous. Or perhaps just afraid of getting another snub, because after that she more or less stuck to yes and no, without the frills.'

'And I see from your report that what it amounted to was that she left the house at six o'clock, having taken a supper tray into the morning-room, where Mrs Laycock was already in bed, watching television. Right?'

'Yes, and that she didn't get home until some time between one and two in the morning.'

'When she went straight to bed and the first thing she

knew about the fire was when she was woken up an hour or two later by her father?'

'Which we'd already heard about from him. Pretty unrewarding, wouldn't you say? You'd have to be a genius to wring any drama out of that.'

'To get back to her father, though; any human touches there?'

'No, none. Very solemn and dignified most of the time and the Coroner didn't have any trouble hearing what he said.'

'Only most of the time?'

'Well, there was just one point where he seemed to flounder a bit. You remember how he was asked about whether he had thought it advisable to leave his wife alone in the house for all that time when, until recently, she'd been ill enough to need a trained nurse to look after her?'

'To which he replied that it was at her own wish that the nurse had left and, although they did their best to ensure that she was never completely alone, it was bound to happen occasionally. In this case, he'd been delayed in London on official business and he had found his wife asleep when he got home. Furthermore, the fire couldn't have started until after that, so he didn't see what the hell it had to do with her being left alone earlier in the evening. Or words to that effect. Doesn't sound very floundery to me. Rather self-confident, in fact.'

'I know, but it didn't all come flowing out like that. There were some hesitations mixed up in it. It was like he'd prepared in advance what he was going to say and then got annoyed with himself for not being word-perfect.'

'Well, I suppose it was because of having to cover up for naughty little Andrea, who'd deserted her post and gone swishing up to London. Anyway, you're very observant, Millie, and that's half the battle. Anything else you noticed?'

'No. Very dull, isn't it? I'd been hoping for a few sinister contradictions and complications to liven it up. That's usually your line, isn't it?'

'I'm taking the opposite one this time. I consider that we

have enough sinister complications with the disappearance of Rosamund Mc Grath to keep us busy for the time being.'

'That's true,' Millie agreed, brightening at the thought. 'That ought to make a good story when it all comes out. And you never know, do you? Perhaps it'll turn out that there's some connection there with the Laycocks. That wouldn't be bad, would it?'

'Not bad at all, and if you do find it, let me be the first to know.'

'There could be another explanation, you know,' Robin said, 'which obviously didn't occur to either you or the news-hound, although I find it equally plausible.'

'Another explanation for what?'

'All of it. The fire and Mrs Laycock's death, as well.'

'But, Robin, since the death certificate states that it was due to smoke inhalation . . .'

'I'm not arguing about that, simply about what caused the fire and why she was the only one to be harmed by it. The jury wrote it off as misadventure and they may well have been right, but you don't like that because of the time lag. So, being you, you plump for murder as the only alternative. Suggesting, in other words, that someone waited until she had passed out and then set fire to the bedclothes.'

'What's your alternative?'

'Why not suicide? If you must have a lurid solution, this one fills all the requirements and it would account for the awkward interval which bothers you so badly.'

'How does it do that?'

'Well, you always assumed that she had only just gone to sleep when Laycock came in at half past ten, but why couldn't she have started swigging from the bottle the moment she was alone in the house? In that case, she might well have passed out by eight, or even earlier. That would have given her five or six hours to sleep it off and then to wake up and realise that, after all the months of struggle, she'd succumbed to the old demon once again and had decided to put an end to the misery once and for all?'

'Funny way to do it, wasn't it?'

'Given her situation and the resources available, what method would you have used?'

'She might have burnt the house down.'

'So she might, but perhaps she had other things on her mind. Still, I can see that my suggestion doesn't find favour. You'd prefer murder any old day.'

'Not at all, and you could be right. It might account for that so-called dream she had. Perhaps she'd been toying with the idea of suicide for some time and wanted to find out at first hand how bearable it would be to do it in this way.'

'Or maybe she did have such a dream, which is what put the idea into her head when she touched rock bottom.'

'Though it still doesn't explain how she got hold of the booze.'

'Which is something we're unlikely ever to know, since a veil now appears to have been drawn over it. However, one can hardly blame Laycock for that. He made no secret of it to Louise, as he surely would have done, if he'd planted the bottle there himself, or handed his wife the keys of the drink cupboard.'

'Unless he invented it, because he thought it would sound more plausible that she should set fire to herself while under the influence?'

'At the risk of bringing suspicion on himself? Well, at the very least, accusations of fatuous irresponsibility. I can't see it.'

'So the question remains: how did she get hold of it?'

'God knows and, if you take my advice, you'll drop this one. The odds are stacked against you.'

'I am unable to drop it for the simple reason that I never picked it up and have no intention of doing so. I have more important matters to contend with. Such as whether that tiresome costume designer is going to push our assistant director in the Isis, or whether she'll pick him up and throw him in first.'

'So you haven't finished the Oxford scenes yet?'

'No, two more days. Sorry about that, but we're badly over schedule, as usual.'

'Which days?'

'Tuesday and Wednesday. I've fixed it with Toby and I'll be back some time on Thursday. From then on, we'll be able to meet quite often, because the following week we move into the studio. Which reminds me of something, Robin. You know that friend of yours, Alan Ferguson?'

'Yes, I am proud to say that I know all my friends. What about him?'

'Have you seen him lately?'

'Not for a month or two. Why?'

'I just wondered if he was due to be invited for a drink some evening.'

'I think I must be dreaming. I could have sworn I heard you say that you had more important things to do than to get mixed up in the Laycock affair?'

'You did and I meant it.'

'And this sudden urge to see Alan has nothing to do with his job?'

'No, it would be all the same to me if he was a professional wrestler.'

'So what's it all about?'

'I'm acting on Elsa's behalf. You remember my telling you about her friend who walked out on her husband and hasn't been heard of since? Well, she has a cousin who is married to someone called Alan Ferguson. We thought it would be fun to find out if he's the same one as yours.'

'In which case, you expect him to be able to tell you where she is?'

'I have no idea what to expect, but when a coincidence like that lands in your lap, the least you can do is pick it up and examine it.'

'Well, I suppose you know what you're doing, or think you do. If I get a chance, I'll try and get hold of him some time tomorrow.'

The decision to keep James McGrath's story to myself had not been arrived at without the sacrifice of a few fingernails. He had not sworn me to secrecy, probably being shrewd enough to realise that it would not have made a blind bit of difference, one way or the other, so I was under no moral obligation to respect his confidence. My instinct had been to pass it on verbatim to Robin at the first opportunity, but reflection had informed me that this could lead to trouble. In the unlikely event of his failing to insist that evidence as hot as this should immediately be passed over to the right quarter, there would still remain the obstacle of his personal reaction. Whether or not he were disposed to believe James's version and to admit that his behaviour could be justified, one thing was certain. I should be nagged to death about taking no part in it myself and to have nothing more to do with the man or anyone connected with him. Promises would be extracted which I did not yet feel confident of being able to keep and it would cause less strain on both of us if I was not called upon to give them.

So I said nothing and was rewarded for this discretion the following evening, when Robin told me that he had spoken to Alan and, since it was not one of my working days, he would be bringing him back for a drink on Monday evening.

On Sunday Ellen and Jeremy came to lunch and afterwards, while the men were watching a cricket match on television, Ellen and I cleared away, scooped the battered remains of bread into two paper bags and sauntered forth to feed the ducks in St James's Park. 'Have you heard the latest about Andrea and Marc?' she asked, as we cast our bread upon the waters.

'No, what's up now?'

'I didn't dare mention it at lunch because I was afraid Jeremy would throw up. He doesn't like Andrea, you see, and he doesn't believe a word she says.'

'Smart fellow! What's the drama now?'

'She and Marc have parted for ever and this time I think there's an element of truth in it.'

'Which is good news, surely? When did you hear?'

'Last night. They were both supposed to be coming for dinner and we'd planned to go on to a jazz club. We never got there, though, because when Andrea turned up, about an hour late, she was on her own and in floods of tears. That was the first thing to send Jeremy up the wall.'

'I'm not surprised. What was her trouble?'

'She kept saying how sorry she was and how she knew she ought not to have come, but she had to talk to someone. She and Marc had had a flaming row, it was all over between them and she hoped never to set eyes on him again. You know how dramatic she is?'

'It takes the wrong form, unfortunately. Did you gather what the quarrel was about?'

'Well, as you can imagine, she wasn't going to let us have it in a few crisp sentences. She went on for about an hour, moaning and rocking about and saying her life was over. Of course, the dinner was ruined, but she told us not to worry about that because it would choke her to eat anything anyway.'

'What a relief for you! What had Marc done wrong?'

'Well, that's where it began to get out of control. Naturally, after such a build-up, she had to find something fairly horrendous to follow it with, but she was in a fix. No black eyes or bruises and I suppose it would have destroyed her image to say that Marc had been unfaithful. She's so colossally vain that she wouldn't want anyone to think that he could even look at another woman. Finally, she fell back on some rather vague accusations of paranoic jealousy, which was pretty feeble and I think that's where the fantasising began to creep in.'

'You know I'd be the last person to take her side, Ellen, but I have to admit that I don't find it so very improbable. He's a most passionate young man, they tell me, and when he goes overboard for some girl he's apt to dive in deep. I can see him working himself into a jealous rage, given the right provocation.'

'Oh, I agree, but it was the circumstances which made it seem so out of character. When I tried to pin her down about what had brought on this fit, she said he'd accused her of deceiving him with another man and what had made it so doubly wicked and cruel was the moment he'd chosen for it.'

'Which moment was that?'

'When he was taking her home after the inquest, would you believe it? When she was already suffering from nervous strain and still in a state of shock about her stepmother's death. Now, that doesn't sound at all like Marc, do you think? No doubt, most of the shock and nervous strain was just an act, but he wouldn't have realised that, would he? So why choose such a time to turn on her, specially when he'd already proved his devotion by giving up the whole day to support her through her terrible ordeal? After all, it's not as though the inquest had changed anything, is it? There was nothing in it to set him off like that.'

'I wouldn't be too sure of that, Ellen.'

'Why not?'

'I have a feeling that it just might have something to do with her movements on the night of the fire.'

'But listen, Tessa, she'd spent the whole evening with Marc. That at least must be true, or even she wouldn't have been dotty enough to have said so, with him sitting there.'

'Unless she'd over-estimated his chivalry.'

'Meaning that she was with someone else that evening?'

'Not exactly. I am sure she and Marc were together for part of it, but I'd be interested to hear his version of this quarrel, if he could only be prevailed upon to give it. The trouble is that I've more or less given my solemn word to keep out of this affair.'

'Which affair?'

'The fire and Mrs Laycock's death.'

'Do you think there might be something fishy about it?'

'I've always suspected there was and now that we have

this new complication I do feel a twinge of regret for having made that promise. Still, I don't see why it should bar me from taking any further interest in the private lives of the Carrington family, do you? I think it might be worth while asking Elsa what she knows about this row between Marc and Andrea. There wouldn't be any harm in that, would there?'

'No harm at all,' Ellen said in her usual agreeable way. 'In fact, I'd call it unnatural if you didn't.'

FOURTEEN

Alan Ferguson arrived on his own a little after six-thirty. He was much as I remembered him, a medium-sized, sand-coloured man, with bony features and a rather defensive manner.

'Good evening,' he said, as I opened the door. 'Is Robin back yet?'

'I'm afraid not, but do come in. I don't suppose he'll be long.'

'I hope I'm not too early?' he asked, following me into the sitting-room.

'Not a bit. I was expecting you and I feel sure Robin must be on his way, otherwise he'd have let me know. What would you like to drink?'

'Whisky, if you have it, with a dash of water. No ice.'

'A true Scotsman,' I said, handing it to him and thinking how considerate Robin was to give me a clear field for a few minutes. Alan obligingly opened it still wider by asking whether I was working at present.

'I daresay that's one of those taboo questions, but I ought to confess straight out that I'm no play-goer. My wife was always wild about the theatre, but it's a year or more now since I set foot in one. Still, always interesting to hear about it from the inside.'

So that gave me the chance to tell him about the scenes we had been doing in Oxford, which in turn led to a description of life at Roakes Common.

'It's in the hills between Dedley and Storhampton,' I explained. 'Do you know that part of the country?'

'Yes, quite well, as it happens. I've done one or two jobs in that area and my wife had a cousin who lived not far off. Village called Sowerley. You probably know it. Have I said

86

something wrong?'

'I'm sorry, I didn't mean to gawp at you, but when you said your wife had a cousin who lived at Sowerley, did you mean that your wife no longer had a cousin, or that the cousin has moved somewhere else?'

'I beg your pardon, I phrased it badly. Grammar's not my strong point. I suppose I should have said that she still has a cousin who still, to the best of my knowledge, lives at Sowerley, but I no longer have a wife. I haven't made it any better, have I?'

'Not much,' I admitted, thinking that, since the odds on a tiny community like Sowerley containing more than one woman who was related to Alan Ferguson must be on the long side, he was squaring up to his recent bereavement with remarkable fortitude.

'My wife and I are separated.'

'Oh, I see! That never occured to me. How stupid!'

'Well, you weren't to know and there's no need to feel embarrassed. It was a mutual arrangement and we parted a year or two ago when my younger daughter was of an age to take it in her stride. We still meet from time to time, though, usually when she has some financial problem which she can't cope with on her own. She's one of those women with no head for business.'

'Not a particularly rare species, but I sometimes suspect that we're under-rated. Getting someone else to do the hard slog might indicate a very good business sense.'

'Is that what you do?'

'Yes, although I don't lumber Robin with it. He hasn't time, for one thing. But tell me about the cousin in Sowerley. I wonder if I've met her?'

'Shouldn't think so. They haven't been there long and Rosamund spends quite a lot of time away from home. Most of her friends are in Sussex, where they lived before. McGrath, she's called.'

'No, I haven't met her.'

'Didn't think you would have. She's a rather reserved sort

of person, not a great mixer. They've no children, which doesn't help, of course.'

'I should have expected that to provide her with more time for mixing, not less.'

'In a sense, but it does rather set her apart from her own generation. I think she feels that it does.'

'Perhaps they should have adopted some?'

'There was some talk of that at one time. She wanted to, but James, her husband, wasn't in favour of the idea and it never came to anything.'

'Did you get on well with him?'

'Oh yes, he's a companionable sort of chap, in his way. He and I always hit it off all right. Used to go away on fishing trips together occasionally, which happens to be something we both enjoyed. It was my wife who disapproved of him. In her defence, I suppose you could say that he's a rather selfish, self-sufficient type and it doesn't bother him that they don't get invited out much by the locals. Probably considers himself a cut above them, anyway.'

'That does sound rather arrogant,' I said, holding out my hand for his empty glass, 'but I suppose the Sowerley crowd must seem very tame compared to sophisticated Sussex society. Whereabouts did they live?'

'Horsham way. Marvellous place they had there too. Beats me why he ever wanted to leave.'

This was good news because I also had relatives in that part of Sussex and, one way and another, the conversation was moving along promising lines. So it was particularly annoying, while I was debating how to take it a stage further without appearing over-inquisitive, to be interrupted by the telephone.

Robin was the culprit and his first words were: 'Did Alan turn up?'

'Yes, ten minutes ago. Do you want to talk to him?'

'No, haven't time. Something's come up. Just pass on my apologies, will you and say I'll make it up to him some day? And listen, Tessa, I'll be back in about half an hour, to pick up a suitcase. Be an angel and rake up something for me to eat.'

'Does that mean you'll be away for the night?'

'At least. Maybe two or three. Can't stop now, though. See you in half an hour.'

'No need to explain,' Alan said, with one of his rare, attractive smiles, when I had put the receiver back. 'I think I caught the gist of it. Sorry to have inflicted myself on you.'

'You've done nothing of the kind, and please don't feel you have to dash away. Tell me some more about these odd-man-out relations of yours.'

It was doomed, of course. The thread was broken and, muttering some excuse about having to make an early start in the morning, he swallowed his whisky and water in two gulps and I was left with twenty-five minutes in which to derive what nourishment I could from the few crumbs of information he had thrown my way.

'And how was Alan? Not put out, I trust?'

'No, he understood perfectly. I imagine it's one of the hazards of his job too.'

'And were you able to glean anything about your missing lady?'

'Not a lot. There were just a couple of oddities which struck me. Have you time to hear?'

'Not now, I'm afraid. I must be off in five minutes.'

'Who are you taking with you?'

'Gilford. He has instructions to bring the car here at eight sharp, so it wouldn't do to keep him waiting.'

'And that's all you're going to tell me?'

'Except for an emergency telephone number. It's on the pad in the hall. I'll call you to-morrow, if I have to be away for more than one night.'

'Ring me at Toby's, then, and leave a message, if I'm not back. I'm working tomorrow.'

'So you are! I'd forgotten. Well, I shan't be far away. Bye, darling. Take care! Oh, and by the way, don't forget to watch the nine o'clock news. It'll tell you as much about what I'm up to as I could myself.'

The third headline related to a story which had been running in the press and on television for several days. I could not understand why Robin should now have a part to play in it, but since it was the only one in the bulletin with criminal associations I paid particular attention as we were briefed on events once again.

On the previous Thursday afternoon in a remote Herefordshire village a seven-year-old boy, the son of a farm worker, had set off on his bicycle after school to ride home for tea, a distance of one and a half miles, and had never been seen again.

Having waited for half an hour past the usual time, the boy's mother had gone out to look for him, taking the road which led between open fields towards the village and, half way along it, had seen the bicycle, undamaged and propped up against a tree. By the time she got home her husband had returned and, on the advice of the farmer he worked for, he had telephoned the police.

A search was organised, which continued throughout the remaining hours of daylight and was resumed soon after dawn on Friday, reinforced by extra men and police dogs. When darkness fell again there had still been no trace of the boy and house-to-house calls in the village and surrounding countryside had proved equally futile. The same pattern had been repeated on Saturday.

On the third day the official search party had been augmented by teams of amateurs. The largest of these consisted of local farm workers, but there was also an assortment of hikers, campers and weekend visitors. This group had included a party of scout cubs and it was they who, on Sunday evening, made what the newsreader now described as the breakthrough.

The territory which had been assigned to them had doubtless been regarded by the authorities as among the least likely to yield any reward. It bordered the edge of a private estate, this part of which consisted of half an acre of recently planted larch trees and magnolias, so situated as to be clearly seen from the house, and it was just inside the boundary that the boys had made their great discovery.

It had come about while they were taking their tea break and had noticed that one of the young trees had wilted and looked near to the point of expiring. With the kindly intention of reviving it, they had climbed over the fence and doused it with a mixture of lemonade and coca cola and, in doing so, their attention had been caught by something else. This was a rectangular patch of turf, of a different shade from the rest, giving the appearance of having been removed at some point and later replaced. An hour and a half later, panting with exertion and excitement, they had arrived at headquarters to report on their findings.

It was by then too late in the day for excavations to be started, but the area was cordoned off and at first light on Monday the spades and shovels had gone into action. Their work had still to be completed, however, when it became clear that orders to call off the search for the missing child would be premature. This was because the makeshift grave did not contain a seven-year-old boy, but a woman five times his age who, as the post mortem revealed, had been dead for over a month.

The telephone number which Robin had written down for me consisted only of numerals, but the first four had a familiar look about them and my guess was verified when I looked up Dedley in the code book.

This, of course, removed the last remaining doubt as to the identity of the dead woman and also explained why Robin had been picked for the job. He had started his career at Dedley as a constable on the beat and had remained there for several years after his promotion to sergeant and subsequent transfer to the C.I.D. So he possessed an intimate knowledge of the local scene, which had resulted more than once in his being in special demand when the regional branch found itself landed with some crime which it had neither the experience nor the resources to deal with on its own.

As it happened, I too possessed some intimate knowledge concerning this case, but I saw no obligation to pass it on. Presumably, now that he was cornered, James McGrath would tell the police the same story he had told me. If not, I should not help either side by doing so myself.

However, sensible decisions reached by logical processes do not always exert any more control over the emotions than those arrived at by the toss of a coin. The temptation to ignore them in favour of the opposite course is just as strong and, having persuaded myself that there was nothing I could do to help or hinder, I found that I could not sleep for thinking about it and wondering how the investigation was proceeding. Needless to say, the knowledge that my alarm had been set to go off at five-thirty, and that a minimum of seven hours' sleep was needed for facing the cameras in the morning, only made the insomnia worse. When the seven hours had been wittled down to six, I gave up the struggle and lifted the telephone.

'I hope I didn't disturb you, Elsa?'

'No, I hadn't gone to bed. Is anything wrong?'

'Could be. Did you watch the nine o'clock news, by any chance?'

'No, Marc's here and we were talking. Have they found that poor child yet?'

'Not yet. What's Marc doing there on a Monday?'

'You may well ask! He came for the weekend and decided to stay on for an extra night. Something on his mind, apparently, but, as he won't tell me what it is, we're not making much headway.'

'Had a tiff with his young lady, do you suppose?'

'Or perhaps just moping because she's gone away for a few days.'

'Has she? Where to?'

'Some friends somewhere in the wilds of Scotland, I gather. It seems the fire and then the inquest on top of it have been too much for her. She had gone into a depression and her father thought it might buck her up to have a change of scene. But listen, my child, you haven't rung me up at this hour to discuss Marc's love life. What's the trouble?'

'I was wondering whether there'd been any developments in the McGrath affair. Whether you or Louise had been able to come up with any suggestions for him?'

'No, complete blank, I regret to say. It's quite obvious from everything we've learnt about Rosamund in the last few weeks that she would never have confided in us about anything of that kind.'

'Have you broken it to him?'

'I tried to. No point in letting him live on false hopes for longer than was necessary, but I can't get hold of him.'

'Why's that?'

'He's away on some job, according to Mrs Baker, who does the cleaning. He'd left a note for her, saying he'd be back some time this week.'

'That's bad news.'

'Well, it's a nuisance, but it will just have to wait until he does get back.'

'I feel I should warn you, Elsa, that you may have rather a long wait.'

'I don't see why. He doesn't usually stay away for more than two or three days when he's on some job.'

'In the meantime, any reactions from the police?'

'Not a murmur. I find that strange, don't you? Specially in view of what Isobel Ferguson wrote in her letter. Still, I'm not complaining. Just thankful to be left in peace.'

'I doubt if it will last. My guess is that they'll soon be buzzing round like flies.'

'Don't be so pessimistic. For all we know, they may have found out where she is.'

'Yes, I'm afraid that's just what they have done and I think this job he's on is quite likely to be in Peru.'

'You're being very tiresome and enigmatic, Tessa! What's it all about?'

When I had told her she was at first too horrified to utter a word, then rallied and began scolding me for believing that anyone we knew could be so wicked. She became so incensed about it that I was afraid it would end with our quarrelling, which would certainly not have improved my chances of a good night's sleep. So I calmed her down by pretending to agree that the woman in the Herefordshire grave was someone neither of us had ever heard of, but I was irritated enough to be unable to resist saying, before I rang off:

'Shall I tell you what I believe is really worrying Marc at the moment?'

'Yes, if you like, but try not to make it too sensational this time. I am not sure I could stand any more.'

I think his trouble is that he does not enjoy seeing the law made an ass of, or himself either, and he is wondering what to do about it.'

FIFTEEN

The dead woman had been formally identified by Mrs Isobel Ferguson, who was then surrounded by television reporters, eager to know how she had felt on learning that her cousin had been brutally murdered. Unfortunately for the viewing millions, her reply had been indistinct.

The owners of the big house and newly planted larch grove were abroad, but their head gardener had been interviewed and, armed with the information he had given them, three detectives arrived at Orchard House on Tuesday morning, with a warrant for James McGrath's arrest on suspicion of murder, only to find that the bird watcher had flown.

'Well, he would have, wouldn't he?' I said to Robin, who had come over from Dedley to have dinner with Toby and myself. 'Presumably, he realised what was liable to happen as soon as they started searching for the boy last Thursday evening and he didn't waste any time. How high do you rate the chances of catching him?'

'Oh, eventually we shall, I daresay. It might take years, but the case won't be closed until we do.'

'In that case, Robin, there is something you ought to know and the time has now come to tell you.'

'Yes, I thought there might be.'

'Oh, how could you have?'

'That faraway look in your eye, I suppose, whenever the subject of Rosamund McGrath came up, and also the fact that you didn't dazzle us with theories about what had happened to her.'

'I'm afraid I was the one to be dazzled this time.'

'By what?'

'Blarney, I suppose you'd call it.'

95

'Okay, so what is it I ought to know?'

'Can you believe that anyone could be so gullible?' I asked at the conclusion. 'I bet you wouldn't have been fooled for a single minute?'

'Yes, I think I might. The D.P.R. probably wouldn't agree, but I don't find it altogether incredible.'

'Well, that cheers me up, but do tell me why?'

'Chiefly because I can't see what advantage there would be in inventing such a tale purely for your benefit. Why take such an unnecessary risk?'

'Not much risk, really. He could always have denied every word, if I'd passed it on.'

'Yes, but why go to such lengths to enlist your help in finding out more about his wife's real or fictitious lover? Surely, any background information you were able to ferret out, such as you tried to get from Alan, for instance, could only have worked against him, if he is guilty? Which reminds me of something else you were going to tell me. How did you make out with Alan?'

'Not very well. He's separated from his wife now, so he hadn't seen Rosamund for over a year. That was a blow, of course, but it also had its interesting side.'

'Really? What was that?'

'Well, according to Isobel's letter, it was he who encouraged her to go to the police, but he made no mention of that.'

'Well, he wouldn't, would he, to a virtual stranger?'

'You don't find it odd that while we were talking about Rosamund he did not refer to her disappearance, or to the fact that his wife was desperately worried?'

'Not if she happens to be the kind of woman who becomes desperate with worry about something or other three times a week.'

'And there was a hint of that, I must admit.'

'I expect he thought she was making one hell of a fuss about nothing and preferred her to nag the police about it, rather than him.'

'I daresay you're right.'

'I am sorry your one small balloon was so easily pricked.'

'Not quite the only one, as it happens. Something else which puzzled me was that he said the McGraths had very few friends in Sowerley. He attributed this to the fact that they, James in particular, considered themselves to be a cut above most people and tended to look down on them. Well, you know, Robin, from what I hear, this is simply not true. Rosamund was considered to be shy and reserved, but it was never suggested that she was snooty and, in fact, she and Louise got on very well. Even Elsa would admit that there's nothing socially or intellectually grand about the Macadams, so that can't have been the attraction.'

'Oh well, you can't expect people to be meticulous in casual conversation, particularly Alan, who doesn't find it easy to express himself. He was probably thinking mainly of James, and Rosamund got tarred with the same brush.'

'Then he was even further off the mark. James was unpopular because of being so pushy and boastful, but there was no arrogance in it. He wanted to be accepted and he seized on every chance that came his way. When you had to back out of Millie's party and Elsa needed an extra man in a hurry, James was the first one she thought of. He accepted with alacrity, despite the fact that he must have realised he'd only been invited because someone else had dropped out. What's more, Elsa never had a qualm about his taking offence, or turning her down. So how do you account for your friend getting it so wrong?'

'I can't and neither, I'm afraid, can I see that it has any relevance to the present situation.'

'Nor can I, as it happens, but you know my motto? There is a place for everything and everything in its place, if only you can find out where it is.'

'Well, you had better apply yourself to it, but please don't expect any help from me.'

'Perhaps I will, when I get time. The fact that you'd have

been inclined to believe James's story has lighted new fires. Still, I'll be up against it, won't I? No use asking, for instance, who designed that larch grove?'

'None at all. It was done by the East Grinstead firm during the time when McGrath was a partner.'

'So, come to think of it, it was an odd place for him to have chosen?'

'Though not so odd, you mean, if it had been chosen by someone else for the express purpose of incriminating him? That's true, but unfortunately, it is also the kind of stupid mistake which any judge will tell you even the most calculating murderer is prone to.'

'All the same, I may not give up just yet. Having backed an outsider, it would be nice to see him come romping home. Perhaps I'll begin by nobbling Louise.'

SIXTEEN

'I hope I'm not disturbing you, Lousie, but I've brought some odds and ends for your jumble sale.'

'How kind of you!'

'Not really. Toby has masses of stuff stored away which he'll never use and Mrs Parkes did the sorting and packing. I'm just the delivery person.'

'I see! Well, thank them both for me, will you? Every little helps.'

'If Tim's around, perhaps he could give us a hand with the boxes? Some of them are rather heavy.'

'No, I'm afraid not. There's a Parish Council Meeting this evening.'

I was aware of this and had my next line ready:

'Oh well, I expect we can manage between us, if we take it slowly. I'll take this one and you lead the way.'

There was nothing she could do about it and when we had each made three trips and I had ostentatiously brushed the dust from my skirt on to my hands, she had no option but to offer me the use of her downstairs cloakroom.

I spent a good five minutes in there, giving her the opportunity to take a peep inside some of the boxes and when I emerged it was a safe bet that she had used it, because she unbent so far as to offer me some coffee.

'Just what I need,' I said, following her into the kitchen. 'Don't go to any trouble, though. Instant would be fine.'

'It was going to be instant, anyway,' she said, switching on the electric kettle.

'Oh, lovely! All right if I sit here?'

'Anywhere you please, my dear.'

'And what about James McGrath? Were you as knocked out as the rest of us by the news?'

'No, I always said he was a scoundrel. Has he been arrested?'

'As far as I know, they haven't caught up with him yet. It can only be a question of time, though, and then the sparks will fly, won't they?'

'Doesn't bother me. All I want is to see him get what he deserves.'

'I know, but Elsa tells me his wife was a friend of yours, so it's bound to be painful for you when all the gory details are being bandied about.'

'I still find that preferable to living with the knowledge that her murderer has got away with it.'

'And of course you'll be able to help things along when you give your evidence.'

The boiling water was coming out of the kettle rather fast and Louise set it back on the stove before replying:

'What makes you think I shall have to give evidence?'

'No getting out of it, I imagine. Having handed that forged letter over to the police, you can hardly expect the prosecution not to make use of it, so it follows that you'll be called as a witness.'

'Here's your coffee. I hope it's as you like it,' she said, not sounding as though she meant it.

'Oh, thanks awfully, it looks marvellous. Some people would be scared into a dither by the prospect of being cross-examined and I am one of them, but I gather you're not?'

'I suppose I am capable of answering a few simple questions.'

'Even if one of them takes the form of suggesting that you wrote the letter yourself?'

'My dear girl, what on earth are you talking about? Why should anyone suggest a thing like that? I never heard such rubbish in my life.'

'Oh well, that's all right then.'

'What do you mean "that's all right, then"? You sit there, making these absurd accusations and then you airily say it's all right. It is far from being all right, let me tell you.'

'Then I apologise, but, you see, Louise, I've been convinced for a long time that it could only have been you who wrote that letter. All the same, I must have been mistaken, otherwise you would never be so stupid as to deny it.'

Getting through her defences had been easier than I had anticipated and I could see that she was now wavering. Putting on a brave show, she said:

'It's too ridiculous for words, but I'd be interested to hear how you came by such an idea. Did Elsa . . .?'

'Heavens, no. Elsa has never made an absurd accusation in her life. No, this was based solely on my own deductions.'

'What deductions, may one ask?'

'Certainly one may and I'll begin by reminding you of a few facts which cannot be disputed. The first is that when you discovered by accident that Rosamund was not with her cousin in London, you went to see James, hauled him over the coals for telling a pack of lies and demanded to know where she was and why she had gone away without a word to anyone. Correct?'

'Perfectly.'

'James eventually admitted that she had left him for another man and gave you the text of a note he claimed she had written to him. Right again?'

'I don't see why you find it necessary to repeat things I know already. There is no secret about them.'

'But it was a secret for a time, was it not? James also told you that he believed this to be just a temporary aberration and that Rosamund would come back. When this happened, he did not want their reunion to be soured by the fact that the story had become the subject of local gossip and he therefore begged you not to repeat anything he had told you. As a woman of principle, you kept your word, not even mentioning it to Elsa. That was how things stood until a few days later, when you received a letter from Rosamund yourself. Naturally enough, since she had not sworn you to secrecy, you considered that you had now been released from

101

your promise. So the first thing you did was to show the letter to Elsa. You agree?'

'I keep saying so, but it still doesn't explain why you should imagine I had written it myself.'

'Well, I've given you the facts and now we come to the assumptions, which are based mainly on the premise that the letter was such an obvious forgery.'

'In what way obvious?'

'Not in the handwriting, which in any case I wouldn't have recognised. It was the style which was the give-away. It was simply not the way in which one woman would write to another.'

'Elsa found no flaw in it.'

'Yes, but we both know how trusting she is and as soon as it was pointed out to her that it might be a fake she suggested as much to you and you told her that you had suspected it all along. That was what first gave me the idea that you had written it.'

'But why me?'

'Because I felt sure that you had not given James your promise without some misgivings. On the other hand, you realised that these could be due to prejudice on your part and you decided to give him the benefit of the doubt. But then, as the days went by and there was still no word from Rosamund, the misgivings grew stronger and you felt that you had to do something positive. You still couldn't bring yourself to break your promise, so you had to find a way to make it null and void and you wrote the letter. It was clever thinking because, if, by some remote chance, Rosamund turned up alive and well and denied having written it, you would have lost nothing. If not, it would provide you with the excuse you needed to bring the police in and you tried to word it in such a way that even Elsa's suspicions would be aroused. You didn't lay it on thick enough, though, and it was sheer fluke that I got to hear about it.'

'Not entirely. She asked me whether I would mind her showing it to you and I gave her every encouragement. I may say that your reaction was exactly what I had been hoping for.'

'So you do admit it?'

'My dear, I admit everything, with one exception. I did not write the letter. I might have done so, if I'd thought of it, I suppose, but I am not so clever as you appear to believe and, fortunately, someone else saved me the trouble. If you've finished your coffee, we can bring this discussion to an end. I have to collect Tim from the Parish Hall in ten minutes.'

'And no doubt you feel it would be prudent to consult him before committing yourself any further?'

'My dear, you really are the most impudent young woman I ever met, and I must warn you that my patience is not inexhaustible. I really cannot see that this is any business of yours, but since you have set yourself up as an inquisitor, I have done my best to humour you. Now, for the last time, I did not forge the letter. Whether you believe that or not is a matter of indifference to me, but I refuse to discuss it further. Is that clear?'

'Oh, clear as daylight, Louise, but it is now my turn to warn you. I mentioned earlier that my conclusions were based on facts as well as assumptions, and there is one fact which you have yet to hear.'

'Oh, very well, if you must, but please try to make it short.'

'Whoever did forge it went to some trouble to disguise his or her own style of correspondence, so some other model had to be found and that's where he or she fell flat on his or her face.'

'What do you mean?'

'I mean that it may not be the way she would have written to you, or any other woman friend, but it was certainly the way she had once written to James. After you'd left him and were thinking over what he'd told you, you doubtless formed the opinion that he had been lying to you about the farewell note, but you were only half right. She had written just such a letter to him two years ago. It made such an impression that he was able to reel it off to you verbatim. Now, what you have to bear in mind, Louise, is that only three people were in a position to know how that first letter was worded. They are the one who wrote it, the one to whom it was written and yourself.'

'Did that do the trick?' Toby asked.

'Oh, she blustered on for a bit, but the fight had gone out of her. I felt a bit mean, to tell you the truth.'

'Better coming from you, I'd have thought, than having it flung at her in court.'

'All the same, there was a trick in it and, if she hadn't been so shattered, she'd have noticed it.'

'Well, I'm not shattered and I haven't noticed it either.'

'She should have pointed out there was a fourth person who could have read the original letter, probably did. He is the one for whose sake it was written and who James believes to be the murderer.'

'My dear Tessa, you're not telling me you believe in this mythical lover figure?'

'Don't you?'

'Not for one minute.'

'Then how do you explain why she was continually darting off on her own for days at a time and claiming to be with her cousin in London?'

'I explain it by pointing out that your informant was James.'

'Why would he have made it up?'

'For the simple purpose of establishing that his wife had a lover. I daresay these trips of hers weren't half so frequent as he now makes out and when they did occur she had simply gone to stay with friends in Sussex.'

'Well, I admit that Alan did say she'd kept up with some of them, but can you explain why James found it necessary to invent such a tale?'

'Like all gardeners, his work was mapped out months in advance. When the season came for Rosamund to disappear, it would be revealed to a shocked community that she has made up this story about being so devoted to her cousin, in order to account for her regular absences from home. What other reason for such deceit than a love affair? With any luck, you will swallow it whole and accept that she has run away with the other man. Failing that, he still has story number two up his sleeve. That was the one he told you and you were willing to believe it, which must have been encouraging for him.'

'In that case, why didn't he stay and brazen it out? Why has he now bolted?'

'Lost his nerve, I daresay and fell back on plan three, only to be used in the direst emergency.'

'So, in effect, you are saying that he not only murdered her, but that it had been planned down to the last detail months or years in advance?'

'Yes, and that's why I considered you were unwise to spend so much time with him.'

'Well, it's not Robin's view and you see what that means, don't you? My two mentors have now taken up their positions at opposite poles. It will not be easy to steer a straight course between them. Why do you keep gazing out of the window while I am talking to you?'

'Because the Carrington girl has been sitting in her car for the past five minutes and it is beginning to worry me. Do you suppose she can have fainted?'

'It is more likely that she is nerving herself to come inside and tell me something I know already.'

'Well, I can see that would take nerve, but why bother?'

'She is not aware that I know it already. The hesitation is due to the fact that she has a problem which she would like to share with me, but fears that by doing so she will be throwing a loved one to the lions.'

'With all that in mind, it would not surprise me if she had fainted. Perhaps you should go and revive her?'

'Thank goodness, you've come, Tessa! I need your advice,

but it gave me the jitters to see Toby glaring at me like that.'

'It has been known to have that effect. Let's go and sit on the tree trunk and let him glare away unseen by either of us.'

'It has heard many confidences in its time,' I remarked, as we walked over the Common, 'including Ellen giving her all when it was the prop for the Round Table. I take it there is an element of chivalry mixed up in this problem of yours?'

'So you've guessed what it's all about? You saw more in my report than I did myself?'

'Not until I heard that Marc and Andrea had had a row. I suppose the truth is that they were together on the night of the fire, but had separated several hours earlier than she chose to tell the Coroner?'

'Right! She said the film had given her a headache and she was going straight home. Well, you know yourself that it doesn't take much more than an hour to drive down at that time of night and he went through the roof when he heard her say she hadn't got home until after one o'clock. The trouble with Marc, though, is that he's so single-minded that he can only ever see the question from one point of view, and it didn't hit him until later that she might have had some quite different reason for lying about it than the one he'd first thought of.'

'And now he's debating what he ought to do about it? The answer, of course, is nothing.'

'Just what I said. I'm glad you agree.'

'And, anyway, what can he do? The case is closed now. He couldn't get it re-opened, even if he wished to.'

'It's not as simple as that, Tessa. He's still dotty about her, you see, and he still wants to marry her. Honestly, don't you often think that sex can be the most awful scourge?'

'Not often, no.'

'Well, it is when it gets otherwise sane and adult people into this kind of mess. One half of him realises that she's an exhibitionist and manic-depressive, to name but two, but the other half says that's perfectly okay. He kids himself that it's all on account of her rotten childhood, her mother dying when she was born and her stepmother being such a wash-out. He thinks she'll be a different character when she has a background of her own and a doting husband to gratify her every whim.'

'Then he'll be able to look out of the window at all the flying pigs.'

'I know and, what's more, I don't believe he gives a damn whether she set fire to her boring old stepmother or not. He'd find some way to excuse it, given time, but that's not his only worry.'

'It would be enough for most people. What else?'

'Well, you see, he's always been hooked on this idea that, whoever else she might lie to, she'd always be straight with him. If only she'd tell him what she was up to during those missing two hours, even if it included murder and arson, he'd pat her head and tell her not to worry, but she won't. She just rants on about how beastly he is not to trust her. If you ask me, she hasn't gone to the Hebrides because she's on the verge of a nervous breakdown, but because she can't stand any more of those reproachable looks.'

'Has he been in touch with her since she left?'

'No. Apparently, these friends she's staying with have a holiday cottage somewhere in the middle of the Atlantic. All very spartan and primitive and the nearest telephone is half a mile away. So far, she hasn't felt strong enough to walk to it.'

'Then how can I advise you, Millie? It sounds to me as though the affair is over and he'll just have to learn to live without it.'

'I thought you'd be able to produce something a bit more inspiring than that to tide him over the worst.'

'Oh, I could reel off half a dozen, starting with the one about his being well out of it, since he could never be sure she wouldn't be seized by the urge to set fire to him one of these days, but it wouldn't do any good.'

'So you do believe she had something to do with it?'

'Let's say I consider her to be capable of it and, if the

107

opportunity happened to turn up when she was in the mood for that sort of game, I daresay she wouldn't have hesitated. There's just one snag.'

'What's that?'

'Self-dramatisation. I bet she was dead scared during the inquest but, having come through that unscathed and finding life a bit of an anti-climax, it would never surprise me if she had now adopted the role of beautiful, Victorian-type murderess. Not to be played on a world stage, mark you, but to an audience of one, who is responding with gratifying attention, one might add.'

'It would still leave all that time unaccounted for,' Millie objected.

'Not necessarily. If she'd arrived home just after her father and gone to her room, as Toby pointed out, she could have found a dozen ways to occupy herself before she started crashing about in the bathroom.'

'So why lie about it?'

'Because at first, if this version is correct, she was anxious for it not to be known that she was in the house between midnight and one a.m. That, you will recall, is the approximate time when the fire is estimated to have started. She could not tell what verdict the jury would come up with, whether there would be suspicion in the air and, if so, who it might fall on. There was even the possibility that the Coroner might think it worth asking her what she had been doing between the time she came home and when she went to bed. But he didn't and, once she was safely out of that wood, the mood changed. Everything had become dull and ordinary again and she thought it would be fun to liven it up by putting Marc through a few hoops. I really believe, you know, that I've talked myself round. After all, I regard that as the most likely explanation for her present behaviour.'

'Not much consolation for my poor little brother!'

'Oh, I wouldn't say that. The role will soon lose its attraction. It's very limiting, you know. Not much you can do to expand and develop it and I daresay that even now, as she sits gazing out over the rain-sodden landscape, she's rewriting the play and casting herself in a new part.'

'So you think we can tell him to stop worrying because your second sight tells you that it's all going to be roses again as soon as she gets home?'

'No, I wouldn't advise that. We might be letting ourselves in for trouble. You're not going to believe this, Millie, but I could so easily be wrong.'

SEVENTEEN

'Two dead females and two missing persons,' I announced, 'or maybe one missing person and three dead females. Could there be a connection?'

'If so, we shall rely on you to find it,' Robin replied. 'Who's the imponderable?'

'Andrea. Missing, but not so far presumed dead.'

'Not in the Hebrides, after all?'

'As her father has now discovered. Being somewhat obsessive about the girl, he got worried when he didn't hear from her, not so much as a postcard to say she wished he was there. He was afraid her depression might have caused her to walk into the Atlantic, which it no doubt would have done, provided the beach was ringed with life guards. Anyway, he sent a telegram.'

'And?'

'She was supposed to go by train to Oban, you see. In fact, he saw her off from King's Cross. It was a night train and she was to catch the boat train the next morning to the island. It leaves at eleven and she was booked into the hotel, so that she could bath and change and so on. When the boat docked she wasn't on board and her name hadn't been ticked off the passenger list. The friends who'd gone to meet her rang the hotel, but she hadn't checked in there either. So they thought "Oh well, that's Andrea for you!" and concluded she'd changed her mind. It wasn't until the telegram arrived that they realised their mistake and that was yesterday, five days after the official E.T.A.'

'What an extraordinary story!'

'Yes, isn't it? Though I doubt if it will have much of a run. She is probably sitting on a beach in St Tropez. Only, of course, that wouldn't sound nearly so romantic and Bronteesque as roaming around in the glens of the Outer Hebrides.'

'So not very seriously missing, you think?'

'I wouldn't rule out the alternative, though. No one could deny that Andrea must have aroused more murderous feelings in those around her than many you could name. How are you getting on with your own missing person?'

'It's a sore subject. Some balm in it for you, though.'

'Why, what's happened?'

'It's more a case of what hasn't happened. We had concluded, you see, mistakenly as it turns out, that McGrath had done a bunk within hours of the first search party setting out to look for the missing boy. The fact that he appeared to have acted so promptly, as though forseeing from the start the dangers that could lie ahead for him, seemed almost an admission of guilt. It strengthened our hand, to that extent, but it also gave him a four-day start and made it that much easier for him to cover his tracks. That all clear?'

'As daylight, thank you, but where had you slipped up?'

'Being so keen to make up for the lost time, we were a trifle over-hasty in setting up the machinery for blocking escape routes and all the other routine business which goes into action for a criminal on the run. We accepted too many assumptions without stopping to verify them.'

'Like?'

'The first report about the boy came on the air at nine on Thursday evening and McGrath had already left Orchard House when Mrs Baker arrived there at nine on Friday morning. The first assumption was that he'd left Sowerley at some point during the intervening twelve hours.'

'Very natural!'

'Yes, well, one of the routine measures I spoke of was to put out a call to garages and filling stations.'

'But nothing came of it?'

'Not a murmur. That's not unusual in the ordinary way, particularly with all these self-service places around. But there's usually someone in charge and on the look-out and, in this case, we might reasonably have expected to jog a memory or two. For one thing, Range Rovers aren't all that thick on the ground and the man who was driving this one is no ordinary type either. Once seen, not easily forgotten, you'd have thought.'

'So, presumably, he wasn't seen and the car is now languishing in some multi-storey place at Heathrow or Gatwick.'

'No, there's another routine measure to cover that sort of thing.'

'How very disappointing for you! But you hinted that I should be pleased by the news and I assure you that I'm not. I have no desire for him to escape your clutches, if he's guilty. I don't want my horse to win by default.'

'You'll do better than that. It's a double triumph for you, really, because the man who really upset the apple cart is none other than your old friend from Fairman's Garage.'

'You mean Owen's brother? Dave?'

'That's the one. It seems he has quite a following in those parts and a number of people take their cars to him for service and repairs, rather than to one of the bigger places in Storhampton and Dedley.'

'Tony included. He's a mechanical wizard, that Dave.'

'Though not very bright in other ways, it could be said?'

'It could, yes. What was he not being bright about this time?'

'He'd heard about our appeal and also a good many other things on the local grapevine, but he hadn't come forward before, because he didn't think we'd be interested. It was Owen who talked him into it.'

'Interested in what?'

'The fact that one day last week McGrath took his car in to be filled up with petrol, have the oil and water checked and all the rest of it. He told Dave to make a thorough job of it because he had a long journey ahead of him. It's all on record in the books because he has a monthly account.'

'Well, that takes the bun! He may not be bright, but he's not a moron either. What can have possessed him?'

'Wait for it! This transaction took place at ten o'clock on Thursday morning.'

It took a second or so for it to sink in and then I said:

'You mean, before . . . ?'

'Exactly! Six or seven hours before the child disappeared.'

'But, Robin, that means . . .'

'That the two events were not connected. Aren't you pleased?'

'Stunned would be the word. What's the official verdict?'

'Hard to define. In a sense, of course, it's pulled the rug from under our feet and we're still reeling from that. On the other hand, it does nothing positive to establish McGrath's innocence and he certainly hasn't come forward to defend himself. The theory now is that he genuinely had planned a trip for Thursday and that somewhere along the way, perhaps on his car radio, he heard the news, changed course and went into hiding. I don't know, though.'

'You don't care for it?'

'Well, it wouldn't have been easy, would it, to hit on a secure hiding place at a moment's notice and get to it without being recognised? Too late by the time the news broke to cross the Channel or the Irish Sea, even assuming that he'd had the foresight to pack his passport.'

'So, privately, what construction do you put on it?'

'On the whole, I subscribe to the view that, as he had undoubtedly organised his trip in advance, he was already in France or Belgium by the time the first news bulletin came out. Since no member of our Royal Family figures in the story, it's unlikely to have got much press coverage on the continent and he probably hasn't seen a mention of it. As I say, it does nothing to prove his innocence.'

'Not in a positive way, perhaps, but it does remove the certainty of his guilt, which is more or less how things stood this time yesterday.'

'With the rider that the story he told you could just possibly be true. Well, we shall soon know.'

'Shall we? How?'

'Because, although the case of a missing child in Herefordshire won't hit the continental headlines, the fact that a man of McGrath's status is wanted for the murder of his wife will make quite a sensation. So, if that's where he is, it can't be long now before he either gives himself up or is recognised and clapped into irons until the extradition papers arrive.'

'I wonder neither of those things has happened already.'

'Me too, but it's out of our hands now. I was only wanted for the Dedley end of things, although I still have a nasty feeling that we've got it wrong and left something out of our calculations which could turn the case upside down.'

'Like the connection I mentioned just now.'

'Which one was that?'

'Two dead women, two missing persons.'

'If you find it,' Robin said, 'be sure and let me know. I'll borrow a helicopter and take you to dinner at Maxims.'

I did not have to endure sleepless nights wondering what to wear for this outing because within hours both missing persons had turned up and the connection remained as insubstantial as ever. Both had a tale to unfold, Andrea's, predictably, being the more improbable and dramatic.

At about the time when Robin and I were discussing hot dinners and helicopters she had wandered into a police station in a south coast holiday resort and announced to the sergeant on desk duty that her bag had been stolen. She had been sitting on a bench in some public gardens, with the bag beside her, when a young man who was passing by seized it and ran off.

At first, she had been too shocked and startled to move or cry out and, by the time she had pulled herself together and approached an elderly couple on a bench not far off, there was little they could do to help her. Realising, however, that she was a stranger to the place and also badly shaken by her experience, they had kindly escorted her to the nearest police station.

Asked for her name and address, she had been able to supply both but further than this she was unable or unwilling to go. She had no idea what she was doing in this town, what its name was, or how she had arrived there. She had a hazy recollection of standing outside a cinema, saying goodnight to someone, but what had happened between then and the moment when she had looked up and seen a young man running away from her, with one arm clasped across his chest, was a complete blank. It was as though the incident had acted as an alarm bell going off in her head and snapping her awake after a long and dreamless sleep.

None of this, however, did anything to delay her rehabilitation, for Gregory, needless to say, had not been idle during her absence. She had already been registered as officially missing and within half an hour he had been summoned and was on his way to collect her. By the same evening she was at home in her own bed, with instructions from her doctor to remain there for at least twenty-four hours. He attributed the amnesia to delayed shock, resulting from the fire and her stepmother's death, and his prognosis was that her memory would return by degrees. On no account should she be urged to try and recapture it.

Matters had not turned out so comfortably for James, but his surrender had also taken place in a police station. This one was in Shropshire, a few miles from the Welsh border and his explanation for being there was as follows:

On the previous Thursday morning he had left Sowerley and driven directly to a cottage he owned in Wales. It was an isolated and primitive sort of place, originally a stone-walled shelter used by shepherds, which he had bought and added on to several years before. He had been drawn to it by the opportunities it offered for bird watching and by the nearby trout stream, in which he now owned fishing rights. He was in the habit of visiting the place several times during the spring and summer, although never accompanied by his wife. Such visits were usually made on impulse and often coincided with periods when she was planning to be away herself.

The recent one, however, had been arranged further in advance than usual. He was expecting a friend to join him there on Friday or Saturday and had gone to some trouble to stock up with provisions and to make sure the cottage was properly cleaned and aired before he arrived.

It had been a wasted effort, though, because the man never turned up and nor did James hear a word from him. This had been an annoyance, but not a totally unexpected one because the friend had a specialised job and was always liable to be called upon at short notice.

He had listened from time to time to news bulletins on his transistor radio and so had been able to follow the progress in the search for the boy. Although it had meant nothing personal to him, his curiosity had been stirred by memories of the landscaping he had carried out so near to where it was all happening. Aside from that, it was just one more depressing news item, tucked away among others which were worse, and on Tuesday he had missed it altogether.

This was because he had by then given up all expectation of seeing his friend and had therefore packed a picnic lunch and spent the whole day fishing, not getting home until dusk. He had listened to a symphony concert while eating his supper and had then read a book until it was time to go to bed, and the news about his wife had not reached him until Wednesday. He had then accepted the inevitable and driven to the nearest police station on the English side of the border.

'How much truth in it?' I asked when Robin had finished telling me.

'Plenty. Everything in the cottage was exactly as you'd expect, if someone had been staying there recently and left in a hurry. Empty food tins, two beds made up but only one slept in, matching tyre marks on the cart track down through the field. Oh, he was there all right.'

'Has he been charged?'

116

'No, the questioning goes on. They've been at it for eight hours and there are probably at least eight more to come.'

'So he hasn't confessed, obviously. Was his story about finding his wife gone, leaving the bloodstained pillow behind her, the same as he told me?'

'In every particular.'

'And you still think it might be true?'

'I suppose I am keeping an open mind about it.'

'Yes, that's the trouble, isn't it? It's so completely incredible that one's instinct is to believe it. What about the friend who never turned up, though? That, at least, must be true because James will have to name him and, if he does exist and can confirm that he had been invited, there'll no longer be any doubt of its being planned in advance.'

'He does exist and he has confirmed it.'

'Oh well, that's something, I suppose, but what a peculiar way to behave! Imagine just not turning up! And then later, when the hue and cry started, why didn't he come forward? I don't understand.'

'You may when you hear who he is.'

'No, really? Who?'

'Alan Ferguson.'

'Honestly, Robin, I can't believe it.'

'Why not? He told you they used to get on pretty well, so long as there were no wives around.'

'In that case, why did he let his old friend down and not bother to tell him that he wouldn't be coming?'

'Knowing Alan as I do, I think it's capable of explanation. He said he ran into McGrath at his club a few weeks ago and they had lunch together. McGrath suggested this trip and Alan fell in with it and made a note in his diary. I expect he had every intention of keeping to it at the time, but . . .'

'But?'

'He now claims that it was only a loose kind of arrangement, not binding on either side and that, when he heard no more, he concluded that James had either had second thoughts, or had forgotten the first one. In other

117

words, it was one of those ideas which go down so well with a glass of port and are afterwards regretted or forgotten. His excuse for not coming forward when he heard that James was wanted by the police is on roughly the same lines. Not having heard from him, he concluded the trip had been cancelled and it did not occur to him that James would have gone there on his own.'

'But you think that's just eyewash?'

'Well, it doesn't quite hang together, does it? The fact that he'd written it down in his diary suggests that the invitation had been given and accepted in rather more definite terms than he now pretends. But, of course, that was weeks ago, before his wife became so worked up about her cousin. I daresay he didn't take that seriously, to begin with, but then, as time went by, with no word from Rosamund, he may have got cold feet. At a guess, he regretted accepting the invitation, but he couldn't very well telephone McGrath and say "Listen, old boy, since there seems to be a lot of talk going around about you having murdered your wife, I'm not too keen to spend a weekend with you in darkest Wales, so do you mind if we call it off?" Instead, he lay low, took no action, failed to call back when his secretary told him McGrath had telephoned and kept his fingers crossed that he would be able to slide out of it, without any fuss.'

'Why not simply have said that he couldn't make it because he had an urgent job coming up?'

'Because things don't work out that way in his line of business. Not many arsonists are considerate enough to give advance notice of their activities. Besides, an excuse of that kind would probably only have led to McGrath postponing the trip to the following weekend, or the one after that.'

'So why didn't he come forward when the corpse was identified?'

'Same sort of reason. He's the type who can't face unpleasantness, tries to shut it out of his mind and hope to God it will go away. This one refused to go away, though, and I'm afraid it looks as though your outsider will lose the race, after all.'

'You did say you had an open mind?'

'Yes, but your trouble is that you equate open-mindedness with being on your side and what it really means is that he is just as likely to be guilty as not guilty and, if it turns out to be the first, it could explain why he singled you out to hear that tale about coming home to find his wife had been murdered and spirited away.'

'How could it do that?'

'Not just because you were a sympathetic audience, or, as Toby would have it, because he fancied you. It's more likely that he wanted to try it out on someone, in case he needed to use it on a later occasion and you had something unique to offer him.'

'What would that be?'

'A degree of expertise, combined with an endless store of curiosity, is how I would describe it. He could depend on you to pick out any flaws and to question him on them and, knowing something of your background, he reckoned on their being similar to the questions he might later have to face from the police.'

'A dry run, in other words? Well, I don't flatter myself that I've made your task any harder for you. Although, I suppose, if you're right and I have helped him to plug up a few holes, it may take that much longer to break him down.'

'And perhaps all you really did was to lend a sympathetic ear to an innocent victim. Time will tell.'

'Time, plus another dip into the endless store' was one reply that came to mind, but I did not say it aloud.

EIGHTEEN

Two days later James McGrath was formally charged with murder and in due course made a brief appearance in a Magistrate's Court, where he pleaded Not Guilty. The hearing was then adjourned and the prisoner remanded in custody until it should re-open in a higher court. Bail was refused.

These facts were reported in the evening paper which Robin brought home with him and he also brought Alan Ferguson, who was able to provide others which had not been printed.

It appeared that they had met by chance, when both were on their way home and Robin had invited him to cash in his rain check, but I thought there might have been an element of contrivance in it too, since the meeting had occured near the newspaper stand where Robin habitually stopped off every evening. Alan, however, was not prepared to admit it.

'Stroke of luck for me, running into your husband like that,' he said, when Robin had gone to fetch the ice for himself and me. 'I wasn't looking forward to spending an evening alone in my bachelor quarters. This news has been quite a knock.'

'Yes, it must be terrible for you and worse still for your wife, I suppose? How is she bearing up?'

'Not well. She always takes things very much to heart, so you can imagine what the last few days have done to her.'

In view of this and of Isobel's reputed dependence on him, I wondered that he should have found it necessary to spend an evening in his bachelor quarters, or to lurk about by news-stands, in order to delay it, but he simply said:

'There's not much I can do for her and she's got our younger daughter home for the school holidays now. I should only be in the way.'

120

'What's her attitude? That James is guilty?'

'Oh, no question about it. There isn't a chance in hell of his getting off, is there?' he asked, as Robin came back into the room.

'Wouldn't know, I'm afraid. Here you are, Tessa, here's yours.'

'I wouldn't call the motive very strong,' I remarked, clinking the ice reflectively. 'I know she was reputed to have money, but he can't be exactly hard up himself and, anyway, he couldn't have touched hers until she was proved dead, which is presumably what he was trying to avoid.'

With his glass halfway to its destination, Alan lowered it again, saying:

'You seem to know a fair bit about it. I was under the impression you hadn't met them?'

'My fault, but you asked me if I'd met Rosamund and I said I hadn't, which was true. I had met her husband, though, and I'd heard the rumours about him. I'm afraid that's why I encouraged you to talk about them. Sheer curiosity and I apologise if you find it distasteful.'

'You mustn't mind Tessa,' Robin told him, 'she takes a burning interest in crime and always hopes that the prime suspect will turn out to be innocent.'

'I see!' Alan said, in the voice of one who had now heard everything. 'Well, personally, I'd give him about as much chance as a snowball in hell.'

'I thought you liked him?'

'Yes, I do, but what's that got to do with it?'

'Just that if you consider him capable of doing a thing like this, without even an overpowering motive to excuse it, it's hard to understand how you can find him likeable as well.'

'Do we know for certain that he had no overpowering motive?'

'Of course we don't,' Robin said. 'Tessa's losing her pedals. If he didn't have one, or at any rate one which he considered overpowering, he'd have to be a lunatic, which seems even more improbable.'

'Or else he's innocent, which James for some reason won't hear of. I just wondered why.'

I had been hoping by this line of attack to provoke him into letting the brake off and now appeared to have partially succeeded, for he said:

'I expect you put it down to prejudice, or my wife's influence and to some extent you'd be right, although perhaps not quite in the way you think.'

'Oh, in what way, then?'

'You're not obliged to answer her, you know,' Robin said, getting up to refill their glasses.

'I know that, but it can do no harm now and it may save her from wasting her sympathy on someone who doesn't deserve it.'

'Well, I'm all in favour of that.'

'You see, Tessa, it's not anything my wife has said that makes me afraid that James may have been driven to do this horrible thing. It's the memory of her own behaviour two years ago.'

'When your marriage broke up? But you told me that was an amicable arrangement?'

'Oh, do let the man get a word in edgeways, Tessa!'

'Okay. Sorry Alan.'

'We're friends, in a detached way, but it wasn't always so. You don't live with someone for twenty years and then quietly agree to go your separate ways. Isobel and I had been drifting apart for years before the final break came. The climax was when I told her I was in love with someone else and wanted to marry her. I wanted a divorce.'

'But she refused?'

'Yes, she refused. Her marriage vows were sacred, or so she claimed, but I did not believe that was her reason. I doubt whether she'd have married me in the first place, without trying to make a good Christian out of me, if she'd felt so strongly about it. Anyway, it was no use trying to paint over the cracks after that, so I moved into a place of my own and that's how it's been ever since.'

I was tempted to ask whether the other woman had moved in with him, but I think Robin must have seen it coming, for he frowned and shook his head at me, so I changed the question to:

'But you're back on friendly terms now?'

'To the extent that we were before and would have remained, in any event. Divorce wouldn't have altered that. She is still the mother of my children and she is still entitled to my advice and support, when she needs them. However, that's not really the point. I seem to have been led away.'

'It happens to the best of us,' Robin assured him.

'My purpose in telling you about my own experience was to point out that a similar situation might have arisen for James and Rosamund. The bitterness and resentment would very likely have been still more intense in his case, since there were no children.'

'Intense enough to drive him to murder?'

'I'm not saying that it did, only that it's conceivable. James is not a man to take kindly to being thwarted, and murder, particularly between spouses, had been committed for less than that, as I am sure Robin could tell us.'

'More often than we ever get to hear about, I shouldn't wonder.'

'Although in this case,' I began, but Alan cut in before I could finish.

'Ah, I can guess what you're going to say. Something about the boot being on the other foot, was it?'

I did not deny it because his question seemed to offer a more promising outcome than the one I had been about to ask and he went on:

'Yes, I've heard some talk about Rosamund being the unfaithful one, but I didn't take it seriously. I could see that some men would find her attractive, but she never struck me as the sort to go in for that sort of thing. Not cold, exactly, but one who had her emotions well under control. Whereas James is the opposite. Full-blooded and vigorous would be one way to describe him. Would you care to hear what I believe to be the true origin of those stories about Rosamund's infidelity?'

'She is not likely to refuse,' Robin said, 'so you had better let me fill your glass.'

'Oh, thanks. Well, I'm sorry to say this, Tessa, but it's my belief James invented them himself, after her death. I don't remember any talk of that in her lifetime and I think they're nothing more nor less than red herrings. You may not agree with me, but I feel sure I'm right.'

'And, if so, it would follow that he killed her, I suppose, but to get back to the point you made earlier, that he might have done so if, like you, he had fallen for someone else and Rosamund wouldn't divorce him. I had been going to say that I don't find that argument very convincing. I can imagine that for some people it might be an obstacle which could lead to thoughts of murder. Where the money was short and there were children to consider, for instance. But none of that applied to the McGraths and surely, in this day and age, a man in that position would simply have left his wife and set up an establishment with his new love. They might have hoped that eventually Rosamund would relent and let him go, but even if she didn't, it wouldn't be such a calamity, would it? Not a matter of life or death?'

'Perhaps not, in most circumstances, but supposing she was much younger than him and wanted to have children? As you've pointed out, unlike me, he had none by his wife, so that could be a big factor.'

'Yes, maybe so.'

'Well, that's for the prosecution to find out. I've only talked about it because you seem to have taken a liking to the chap and want to see him acquitted, and I was hoping to spare you disillusionment.'

'Very considerate of you,' Robin said, 'and perhaps Tessa has now plagued you enough. Why not come and have dinner with us? There's quite a decent Italian place round the corner.'

However, the risk of further plaguing, to accompany the

ravioli, may have loomed more threateningly than the prospect of spending a lonely evening in his bachelor quarters, because he soon afterwards left.

I can't imagine why you should make such accusations,' I complained. 'It seemed to me that he took most of the initiative. Once started, there was no stopping him.'

'I hope you found something of value in it?'

'Quite a lot, and what interested me most was why, having professed to like James, he should go to such trouble to work up a case against him. I know he gave an explanation of sorts, but it wasn't very convincing.'

'I agree and I think the truth is at once more simple and more complicated.'

'Just the kind of mixture I like. What are the ingredients?'

'Somewhere at the back of his mind there's probably a nagging feeling that he did James a bad turn by opting out of that trip to Wales. Obviously, it wouldn't have made any difference if he had gone, but it may now seem like kicking a man who was down, and you know how it is when you feel you've played a shabby trick on someone? You start inventing all sorts of reasons why it was their fault and why, anyway, they weren't worthy of your time and trouble.'

'Yes, I suppose that would explain it.'

'Unfortunately, it does nothing to help your crusade to save an innocent man.'

'I don't know that he's innocent, do I? Besides, it's all grist to the mill, to use one of your own expressions. And that wasn't the only point of interest either.'

'No?'

'No, another popped up when he was talking about Rosamund. He described her in a way which I never heard anyone do before. He said she was attractive.'

Robin did not look much impressed by this, so I did not mention something else that had been said about Rosamund, though privately resolving, just to keep my hand in, to find some way to follow it up.

NINETEEN

Two of next morning's papers carried another item of interest to Sowerley readers, the announcement of Andrea Laycock's engagement to Marc Carrington.

Elsa sounded very chuffed about it when I telephoned to congratulate her, but she either did not know or wasn't telling how this reconciliation had come about, so I next applied to Ellen, who was scarcely more informative.

'Since I only have Andrea's word for what the quarrel was about in the first place, I'm in no position to tell you how they made it up.'

'But Daddy has relented, presumably, and given them his blessing?'

'Must have. At any rate, he's coming to their engagement party.'

'How do you mean, "coming to it"?'

'We're giving it here. He said it wouldn't be suitable to have it at their house so soon after step-mama's death and of course it would never do for the bridegroom's family to step in. That would be a breach of etiquette, so Andrea asked if we'd lend them the flat for the evening. Most of their friends are in London, anyway, so it makes sense.'

'Bit of a headache for you and Jeremy, though?'

'Oh, it doesn't bother me; and Jeremy, who's a chip off the cunning old Roxburgh block, says there's nothing to stop our papering the house with a few of our own friends and letting Gregory foot the bill for them too, since he's getting off so lightly.'

'So it's a slap-up do, is it?'

'About sixty, so far. Marc and Andrea are coming here this evening, to draw up lists. Listen, Tessa, if you're so quizzy, why don't you and Robin come too? We can pretend we need Robin's advice on how to get special parking dispensation.'

'I don't think it's quite in his line and, anyway, I know he wouldn't be able to come. He's working flat out on something at the moment and doesn't get home before nine or ten.'

'Okay, come on your own. We can make it look as though you'd just popped in unexpectedly.'

'I might do that. What time?'

'Sevenish. We ought to be through with the organising, by then.'

'Right. See you around seven.'

'Hope I'm not interrupting anything?' I asked, making it look as though I'd just dropped in unexpectedly.

'No, we've been discussing plans for their engagement party and now Marc and Jeremy are going to work out which furniture will need to be moved out of here and which of the other rooms it can be stacked in. I must look for a tape measure. You know Tessa, don't you, Andrea?'

'Of course I do. How are you?'

'Fine, thanks, and glad to have found you here because now you can tell me all about the wedding. Have you fixed the date yet?'

Never one to hang back when there was a chance to talk about herself, Andrea tinkled away without pause for several minutes, prefacing her remarks about who would design her dress, the number of bridesmaids and the hotel where the reception would be held by explaining that none of this splendour was of her own choosing. She would have preferred to slip quietly off to the registry office and cut out all the fuss, but Daddy wouldn't hear of it. It was he who was insisting on the full ceremonial splash.

This, if she was speaking the truth for once in her life, disposed of one question and another also received an oblique answer not long afterwards when I asked:

'So you've lost your ambition to become an actress, I take

it? Or do you mean to pick it up again after your marriage, when you'll be out of your father's jurisdiction?'

'An actress?' she repeated, in a wondering voice.

'Yes, you seemed to be dead keen on the idea at one time.'

'Did I really? I don't remember . . . I'm sorry, but you must excuse me . . . I'm suffering from amnesia, you see.'

'That must be annoying for you!'

'Yes, it is. It makes everything so frantically awkward. People keep saying things as though they expect me to understand and half the time I haven't any idea what they're talking about.'

'Very confusing, but I expect your memory will come back gradually, if you're patient with it.'

'No, it won't,' she said with unusual firmness. 'The doctors thought so at first. They thought it would only take a few days, but they were wrong and now they say there's no hope at all. It's really scary having this huge gap in your life that you know nothing about.'

'Must be, although I suppose it has certain advantages too?'

'Not that I've noticed. Why do you say so?'

'It occurred to me that one says and does a few silly things practically every day of one's life, so the huge gap at least frees you from wishing some of them undone and unsaid.'

'Oh . . . oh yes, I see what you mean. God, is that the time? Where's everyone gone? Marc and I are supposed to be at the theatre in twenty minutes.'

'Don't panic!' Ellen said, coming back in to the room, 'Marc has everything under control and the taxi is on its way. Although, as a matter of fact, the address he gave them on the telephone was some restaurant in Soho.'

'Oh, did he? How stupid of me! I'm afraid my poor old memory still gets a bit tangled up sometimes. It's lucky I have someone as efficient as Marc to take care of everything.'

'So that's the game, is it?' I asked, when Ellen and I had moved on to the kitchen, where she was now dousing escalopes in egg and breadcrumbs with the speed and precision of a machine on a conveyor belt. 'I suspected it all along. Have you and Jeremy developed the most enormous appetites, or were you so farsighted and thoughtful as to buy enough for me?'

'It didn't need thought or foresight. You told me Robin wouldn't be home before nine or ten, so it was as good as done. Which game are you talking about?'

'Amnesia, as played according to the rules of Andrea Laycock.'

'You mean she's cheating? I'm not at all surprised, but how can you tell, Tessa? If someone says they don't remember something, it's not easy to prove that they do.'

'Sometimes it is and probably the only honest thing she said the whole evening was that her memory still gets tangled up at times. Never a truer word! She got herself into a right old tangle with her opening remark. You reminded her that we'd met before and she agreed, without a second's hesitation. Admittedly, that was before the loss of memory is supposed to have set in, so she was quite right not to pretend she didn't recognise me.'

'Okay, so where did she go wrong?'

'Later, when you were out of the room. She claimed to have no recollection at all of wanting to become an actress. Well, the point is, Ellen, that at neither of our two previous meetings did we touch on any other subject. She talked exclusively about herself and the theme was her ambition to break into television. You doubtless remember the first occasion and on the second she explained at length why she had been forced to drop it. So I ask you! How could she have remembered me so clearly and yet retained no recollection whatever of what we had talked about? And I'll bet you anything she'd begun to realise her mistake towards the end. She looked quite terrified at one moment and that was when she became in such a frantic hurry to get away.'

'Although Marc had already rung for a taxi,' Ellen pointed out.

'I know. Naming an entirely different destination from the one Andrea had mentioned. But then, you see, he'd probably been in a frantic hurry to get away ever since I did my dropping in accidentally bit.'

'Why would that be?'

'Most likely because he still sees me as the ten-year-old babysitting ogre, who thwarted all his Machiavellian gambits to stay up half an hour past his bedtime. He's no imbecile and he must have seen through Andrea's little deception. He's pretending to believe it, though, as a face saver, because he's so cracked about the girl that he'd stoop to anything rather than lose her. The last thing he wanted was for me to come barging in and rock the boat by catching her out.'

'I expect you're right, Tessa, but what puzzles me is why she should bother to play the game at all. Is it because she hasn't the brains to invent some plausible excuse for Marc about the missing three hours, or is it just another attempt to make herself interesting?'

'I'm not sure, but I have a feeling that this time there might be a bit more to it than either of those. She was really jittery this evening. It gave me the impression that she knows something which she is either trying to force herself to forget, or of someone realising she knows it and trying to drag it out of her.'

'About the fire, you mean?'

'About the fire and perhaps about other things as well.'

TWENTY

Rosamund had made a new will only a year before her death, which, in the view of some, augured badly for James, since, apart from a few minor bequests, she had left everything to him.

Five thousand pounds and various items of jewellery went to her cousin Isobel and the local rural preservation society also benefited to the tune of five thousand. However, I regretfully abandoned the idea that Tim and Louise, dedicated though they were to the cause, had conspired to murder her, in order to get their hands on this windfall.

All these bequests, along with the bulk of the estate, were naturally subject to probate, but James had sent Isobel a message through his solicitor, requesting her to go to Orchard House as soon as possible, to sort out Rosamund's clothes and personal belongings, taking anything she wanted for herself and disposing of the rest as she saw fit. He also wished her to arrange for the house to be put on the market.

Isobel, however, declared herself to be quite unequal to either of these tasks, vowing that nothing would induce her ever to set foot in the place again and, despite some opposition on his part, had prevailed on her semi-detached husband to undertake them for her.

His protest that he would not have the faintest notion how to set about the first of them had been countered by her advising him to appeal to Elsa and Louise and she had telephoned them both, to enlist their help.

'He's coming down tomorrow,' Elsa told me, 'so he's not wasting any time. Poor James! I suppose he also feels that he could never set foot in the place again, even if he's acquitted. I'm not madly keen to set foot in it myself, to be honest with you, but it has to be done.'

'I imagine you're not the only one and it's going to make it rather hard to get rid of, isn't it?'

'Almost impossible, one would have thought. The minute any potential buyers show up, they'll hear the whole gruesome story and it's bound to put them off. At any rate, that's what Louise is hoping.'

'Why? Would she prefer it to remain empty and at the mercy of the vandals?'

'No, she's got her eye on it for some friends of hers, who want to move out of London. They're a young couple, with small children, so she thinks it would be ideal for them and they'll be able to get it at rock bottom price.'

'How could anyone be so callous?'

'No, just practical. She says that, once it's re-decorated, with all their own furniture in and the children scampering about, the ghosts will be exorcised. As she sensibly points out, there can't be many houses of a hundred years old or more where something dreadful hasn't happened at some time to someone. The only difference is that you don't usually know about it, so it's silly to be squeamish just because you do.'

'Well, personally, if I were thinking of buying it, I'd expect to have another ten thousand knocked off the price, as compensation for having to live within hailing distance of Louise.'

'Well, now, Tessa, I am sorry to hear that because I was going to ask you to do us a favour.'

'Go ahead!'

'Now that you've finished your studio work, I was wondering if you'd come down for the day and give us a hand?'

'With sorting out Rosamund's belongings? I don't think I'd be much use to you there.'

'No, we shan't need your help with that, but I've been thinking. Mr Ferguson will be arriving at ten, but we can't possibly get through till late afternoon. So that means giving

132

him lunch and it's going to be a bit sticky. One can't very well turn it into a social occasion and invite other people. For one thing, they probably wouldn't go away. On the other hand, I don't relish the prospect of sitting through lunch with him when he and I and Louise have spent the whole morning together and have nothing to look forward to but the whole afternoon. I thought, if you were there, it might brighten things up a bit.'

'And we could explain that I'd just happened to drop in unexpectedly?'

'Something like that. After all, you tell me he's an old friend of Robin's, so that would make a sort of bridge and give us something else to talk about. Do you think you could?'

'But of course, Elsa! I shall look forward to it and it will provide a counter-irritant for Louise.'

'They could do with another five minutes,' I said, sticking a fork into one of the potatoes in the bottom oven, while Elsa busied herself with the assorted cold meats and salad.

'Good! Give us a chance to relax and have a drink. Alan's got his whisky and water, so we don't have to worry about him. Is wine all right for you?'

'Wine would be fine. How's it going at Orchard House?'

'Not badly. Very exhausting, though, and it's taking much longer than I expected. Thank God for Louise! It would take me a week to do it on my own, without her to organise everything. All the same, it's quite a relief that she decided to go home for lunch. She wouldn't approve of our lazing about like this, when there's work to be done. If I know her, she'll swallow a cup of tea and a biscuit and get back on the job.'

'In what way does she organise you?'

'Into our separate functions. She's taken on the bedroom and bathroom and I'm doing the kitchen. We have to sort everything into three piles, one to be thrown away, one for Oxfam and the rest for the village jumble sale.'

'And Alan?'

'Oh, he's dealing with all the papers in Rosamund's desk. Very tedious it must be, too, but at least he's able to sit down.'

'I thought that was the executor's job?'

'He is the executor. One of them, that is, the other being James.'

'So when do you expect to be through?'

'Oh, some time tomorrow, with any luck. Louise and me, I mean. Alan's going to attack the garage later this afternoon and them he'll be off. He's leaving the keys with Louise, so that we can finish in our own time and also so that she can show the estate agents over.'

'And point out all the defects, so as to be sure of her friends getting it nice and cheap.'

'I intend to make you pay for that remark, Tessa.'

'How?'

'I told you there was nothing for you to do up there, but, having seen what lies ahead, I think there might be one small job you could take on. On second thoughts, I'd better wait and tell you over lunch, in case Alan has any objection. He's nominally in charge and one wouldn't want to step on any toes. I'm sure those potatoes must be ready by now, so let's make a start, shall we?'

Alan had no objection and nor had Louise, who, as had been foretold, was already hard at work, having temporarily transferred her activities to a small work-room on the top floor. An electric sewing machine, ironing board and typewriter were stacked against one wall, already labelled for their destination. And she had now turned her attention to an assortment of needlework in varying stages of completion. She explained that she had taken the opportunity to deal with these items while Alan was out of the way, so as not to be in it when he resumed work on the desk, which was also in this room.

'Very kind of you, Tessa! We could certainly use an extra

pair of hands, but you'll need an overall. Now, let's see what we can find for you among this lot.'

I could guess the reason for this unusual affability because the task they had allotted to me was to clamber up a frail-looking steel ladder, through a square hole in the ceiling into the loft and to make an inventory of its contents. Apart from being an uncomfortable and dirty way of spending an afternoon, a glance at the entrance was enough to show that neither she nor Elsa could have squeezed through it without first going on a crash diet.

'I put my head inside to see what was there,' Lousie went on. 'It seems to be mostly fishing tackle and raquets and so on, but there are some suitcases as well. They may all be empty, of course. Let's hope that some of them are because it would simplify our job down here, but that's for you to find out. Have you got a pencil and pad for her, Alan? And no smoking, mind! We don't want another fire, to add to our problems. You'd better leave your bag down here, in case you get tempted.'

'The light's on already,' I said, peering up. 'How come?'

'Because the switch is down here, over by the door. All set now? Right! Then up you go!'

I started by making an inventory of the fishing rods and other sporting paraphanalia, then tested each of the suitcases for weight. Four were obviously empty, so I carried them over to the other end of the loft and placed them around the square hole. Of the three which remained one contained nothing but gum boots, mackintoshes and heavyweight jerseys, the second was locked and the third filled with photographs. So I knelt down and spent a happy forty minutes browsing through them.

Many were framed or pasted into albums, but some were loose in envelopes, and the bottom layer consisted of several dozen more, wrapped in the yellowing pages of an old newspaper.

Wondering yet again why yesterday's paper should be

135

practically unreadable, when it is destined in only a few months to exert such fascination, I looked closer and found that this one was no exception. It was part of a two-year-old copy of the *East Sussex Mercury and Gazette* and my eye was instantly caught by a headline which stated: 'TREE FELLER DROPS "HOT" POTATOES'. This was irresistible, so I opened a folding canvas chair, removed the lighter and packet of cigarettes, which I had had the foresight to place inside the pocket of my jeans, and settled down for a good read.

'Strange,' I thought some ten minutes later, as I extinguished the cigarette and flattened the stub underfoot, 'how ironical life can be!'

I had never had the least doubt that both Alan and Louise had so arranged matters as to give themselves the opportunity to make a private and thorough search through the writing desk. There was no doubt, either, that both had been inspired by the hope of coming upon a secret drawer, or finding some clue to Rosamund's love life tucked away among the milk bills and bank statements. Whereas, if they had only put themselves to the trouble and discomfort of climbing up to the loft, a real prize might have been theirs for the taking.

However, there was no time to dwell on these solemn reflections because, while I was re-folding the chair, I heard a sound composed of a mixture of bumps and scrapes coming from the far end of the loft and, turning round, saw one corner of the wooden plank sticking up and swaying back and forth, then moving sideways to fall into place with a whack and completely cover the hole. Two seconds later the light went out.

Mindful of the fact that whoever was responsible for this outrage might have second thoughts and push the lid up again at the very moment when I was standing on it, I took the precaution of crawling over to it on my hands and knees. Having found it and pushed it to one side, I lay flat on my stomach, with my head dangling through the hole into the room below. It came as no surprise to find that it was empty, or that the ladder had been moved out of reach and the door closed. On the credit side, there was now at least enough light to enable me to find my way back to base and to replace everything in the suitcase, with the exception of one page from the newspaper.

Having made the return journey to the exit once more, I peeled off the particularly hideous dress which Louise had selected as an overall, and threw it overboard. Then I swung my legs through the hole, twisted round and hung for a moment or two, measuring the distance, before dropping unharmed to the floor. It only remained to transfer the folded page to the inner compartment of my bag and to make my way to a bathroom where, for the second time in a week, I stood in a strange house, scrubbing the dust and grime from my hands.

'What in the world possessed him to do such a thing?' Toby asked when I had given him a graphic account of my narrow escape, having dropped in unexpectedly on my way back to London.

'I really couldn't tell you. He claims it was a misunderstanding and he was full of apologies. It seems that he'd been in the garage and came back to the workroom to fetch his jacket. He didn't hear a sound from the loft, so concluded I'd finished the job and come down. To be fair, I was keeping pretty quiet at that point. He also claims that he did give a shout, but if so it must have been a muted one, because I certainly didn't hear it.'

'Very thin, if you ask me.'

'And I might add that he was on the point of driving off when I made my reappearance, and Louise of course had returned to her proper territory on the first floor as soon as I was despatched to the loft, so there wasn't a soul within earshot. If it hadn't been for that daredevil leap to freedom, I might have been stuck up there for hours.'

'Quite extraordinary! What had you done to annoy him?'

'Ah well, that's the question, isn't it? But I shan't attempt to answer it now because I have something more interesting to tell you. I believe I have found the link.'

'Oh, good! I shall try not to snap it. What link?'

'Just take a look at this,' I said, removing the wad of paper from my bag, 'and tell me what you make of it.'

'I make less than nothing of it,' he confessed a few minutes later. 'It appears to be a fulsomely worded article about some people called Fitzherbert having generously thrown open their magnificent garden, to raise money for the nurses.'

'That describes it perfectly. Now look at the photograph. What do you see there?'

'I see two men and two women standing together in a magnificent garden. The caption tells me that it portrays Colonel Fitzherbert chatting to Mr James McGrath, the designer of the new aviary and water garden. I therefore assume that the old woman is Mrs Fitzherbert and the younger one, hovering on the fringes, Mrs McGrath.'

'Yes, of course, I forgot you'd never met her.'

'Neither did you.'

'I am not talking about Rosamund. The hoverer in that photograph is Andrea Laycock.'

'Are you sure?'

'Certain. At first, like you, I assumed she was James's wife. It's a bit blurred, but still there is something about the way she is looking at him which gives the impression of two people who know each other well. When I looked closer I saw that it was Andrea.'

'Well, that clearly is a link and not one I should have found easy to snap. Nevertheless, I am baffled.'

'By what?'

'The light of triumph in your eye. It does not seem to be the sort of link to do much for your crusade to save James McGrath.'

'Or to halt it either. There is no setback in the discovery that he had a mistress. I daresay he's had plenty in his time.

138

The fact that we now have grounds for believing that at some point in her past Andrea was one of them doesn't prove that he murdered his wife.'

'Then what does it prove?'

'I have no idea, but it must have some significance, although not the one you imply. He certainly could not have killed Rosamund in order to marry Andrea.'

'Why not?'

'Because we know for a fact that she is going to marry Marc.'

'One could argue that he has a slightly more secure future.'

'Yes, one could, and I wouldn't put any shabby trick past that one, if she saw it as a way of getting herself out of trouble, but when she first took up with Marc no one knew that Rosamund was even dead. Besides, why would she need to marry anyone? She is in no danger of being implicated.'

'You are deceiving yourself, Tessa.'

'Why do you say that?'

'It was the wrong word. I should have said that you are being stupid, blind and arrogant.'

'Well, I'm glad you didn't; I prefer the wrong word.'

'The tiresome man flattered you and you fell for it. You have now become obsessed with proving yourself right and everyone else wrong and you are starting to twist the facts into a form which suits you. Shall I tell you how I interpret them?'

'Go ahead!'

'James and Andrea meet and fall in love. They wish to marry. Andrea will not have him on any other terms and Rosamund will not let him go. When James breaks up with his partnership in Sussex he sets up a new business here because he thinks it will make it easier for him to see Andrea and keep in constant touch with her. It also has the advantage of removing Rosamund from all her former friends, to whom she will frequently wish to return, and in which he gives her every encouragement. This at least allows him spells of freedom to spend time with Andrea, but it is not enough. Andrea is becoming restless. It has begun to dawn on her that she is wasting her youth on someone who is unlikely ever to be in a position to marry her. The final blow falls for James when he sees how things are building up between her and Marc, who is not only young and well off, with the chance of a brilliant career ahead of him, but, most important of all, is not encumbered by a wife. He decides that only Rosamund's death can release him from this intolerable situation. How about that?'

'All right, as far as it goes. It would account for some of the facts, but there are a lot you've left out.'

'Then allow me to finish. Having disposed of Rosamund, James hits on the clever idea of telling everyone, including Andrea, that she had left him for another man. He also tells everyone, with the exception of Andrea this time, that he is hoping she will come back. Andrea is not in love with Marc and nor is she indifferent to James. The prospects of being able to marry him and have a family are looking brighter and, being the unstable creature she is, she is now inclined to switch back to him again. Which brings me to the night of the fire.'

'Oh, you've worked that in too, have you?'

'Indeed I have and I must tell you that, not for the first time, you have tried to make everything too complicated. Naturally, it has now become of vital importance to James that their relationship remains secret, so ways and means of meeting are just as hard to come by as ever. Hard, but not impossible, however, and on the night of the fire Andrea, who has been spending the first part of the evening with Marc, tells him that she has a headache and will drive herself home and go to bed. She does nothing of the kind. She drives herself to Orchard House and stays there until after one o'clock. I need hardly say that it never entered her head that she would be called upon to account for those missing three hours, either to Marc, or her father, or anyone else. Having to do so under oath, in a Coroner's court, must have been punishing indeed. Still, I daresay there was an element of excitement in it too, a touch of the dangerous living which would have appealed to her. How am I doing?'

'Not bad, so far, I am bound to admit. How about the amnesia, though? Can you find a place for that?'

'With the utmost ease. Andrea never had the faintest intention of spending five minutes in a lonely cottage in the Hebrides. Her destination all along had been a lonely cottage in Wales. She and James meet by arrangement at some railway junction and he drives her the rest of the way, arriving after dark. When he hears that a dead woman had been found in Herefordshire, he realises that there is not a moment to lose in getting Andrea away. No time for elaborate plans, so they fling together this story about the amnesia. He drives her, again under cover of darkness, to the nearest large town, where she registers at an hotel under a false name and the next morning she begins the journey which will end on a park bench in a seaside resort. By this time she has conveniently remembered who she is and where she lives and within twenty-four hours of scurrying away from the sinking ship, has announced her engagement to Marc Carrington. She knows that James will never betray her. To do so would only make his motive all the stronger. There now!'

'I don't know, Toby. It covers a lot of the ground, but not all. For instance, for how long did James imagine he could keep up the pretence that he and Andrea would be able to marry? He must have known that this could only happen when there was proof of Rosamund's death, which is the last thing he'd have wanted.'

'I am not a magician and I can only tell you how things were up to the time of his arrest, not what he had in mind to do, if that had never happened. My guess is that he was so infatuated with the silly creature that he did not try to see further ahead than a week or a month. He simply snatched what he could, while he could.'

'And you haven't produced any explanation for the fire.'

'Oh, that fire! How you do go on about it, Tessa! Why ever can't you accept the official verdict that it was an accident? Why do you always think you know best? It's becoming a fixation.'

'Most people do think they know best. The only difference is that I admit it.'

'Thinking doesn't make it so and, in this case, I consider you are foolish to admit it. However, I see that I have not convinced you. I suppose it would take more than rational argument to do that.'

He was becoming so tetchy about it that I pretended to be half won over. It was not true, however, for I had noticed several omissions and discrepancies in his rational argument. One of the more serious, in my view, concerned Alan Ferguson's invitation to the Welsh cottage. Admittedly, he now claimed this had never been confirmed, but he had made a note of it in his diary and the fact that James had also remembered it must surely have meant that he was prepared for Alan to turn up. In which case, he would hardly have made an assignation with Andrea for the same weekend.

Furthermore, I had seen the look of terror in her eyes when she realised the mistake she had made in her memory sequence. If it was true, as, in any event, it had to be, that she felt herself to be in no danger of betrayal by James, then who or what was she so afraid of?

One way to get the answer might have been to find out how, in fact, she had spent those lost five days. Unfortunately, since it was obvious that she would henceforth do her utmost to keep out of my way, it was going to take a bit of doing. I decided to begin, as usual, by consulting Ellen.

TWENTY-ONE

'Where would someone of her age and background be most likely to spend five days of her life and afterwards declare herself to be unable to remember a single moment of them?' I asked. 'Just reel off a list of places that occur to you and we'll see which one best fits her temperament.'

'Only two come to mind,' Ellen replied, having considered the matter, 'and I should say that they both fit her equally well.'

'Not a bad start. What are they?'

'The most obvious one is that she was with some man, although presumably not the one she is now going to marry.'

'Yes, that idea had already been mooted and, in my opinion, found wanting. Let's hear the other.'

'She's already been away on some weekends of that sort and consequently had to spend a few days in a private nursing home.'

'Well done! But would it really take as long as that?'

'It might, if there were complications, or if she'd let it drift on a bit too long.'

'Which, with her mentality, is most likely what she would have done. Yes, that fits splendidly. I suppose you wouldn't have any idea who the father of this embryo might be?'

'No, sorry, none at all.'

'Pity! Still, it's a handful of grist, I suppose, and clever thinking on your part.'

Ellen shook her head. 'It was Andrea herself who gave me the idea.'

'Oh, no! Don't tell me she actually admitted this was what brought on the amnesia?'

'No, but the other day she was telling me about a similar sort of incident in her murky past. Only that time it turned out differently because she really had let it run on too long. Abortion was out.'

'So what happened?'

'She went into hiding until the baby was born. Her father fixed everything and arranged for it to be adopted.'

'I find it hard to understand how anyone could go into hiding for five or six months, without being recognised by someone, somewhere. What did she do? Sail round and round the world on a cruise liner until she went into labour?'

'No, her father rented a cottage for her somewhere near Newquay, where the baby was born. He went down to see her as often as he could and she had her old Nannie there to look after her.'

'And she told you all this only the other day? Why?'

'She was working up to the big scene, where she confessed all to Marc. She asked me whether it would be fair to marry him, if she didn't.'

'And what was your advice?'

'Not to say a word about it, either now or in the future. For one thing, knowing Andrea as I do, there is no guarantee that she hadn't invented it. And telling Marc could only mean disaster. It certainly wouldn't put him off wanting to marry her. In fact, our little St George would probably be all the keener to make it up to her for all the nasty dragons in her past.'

'And you have no idea who the father was?'

'No, she didn't mention him.'

I sighed, wondering how it would feel to have been born like Ellen and to go through life minding my own business.

'Well, I know it goes against your grain, but, if the subject should come up again, do try and find out a bit more, will you?'

'Okay, Tess, I'll do my best.'

'Thank you, darling and, with those words ringing in my ears, I'll be on my way. Unless there's anything I can do to help you get ready for the party?'

'Oh, no thanks. I don't suppose I'll need to lift so much as an ice cube. Marc has laid on the same caterers as they had for Millie's birthday. I suppose there's no need to ask if you'll be coming?'

'No need at all. Six to eight-thirty, did you say?'

The chip off the old Roxburgh block had not only packed in some of his own friends, but had also been thoughtful enough to invite a sprinkling of mine, one of whom was my agent. This was a mixed blessing because, although it is always a pleasure to see her, if she has a weakness, it is her inability to detach herself from professional preoccupations. No matter what the surroundings, given quarter of a chance, she contrives to transform them into an extension of her own office.

On this occasion I had scarcely set foot in the room before she had backed me into a corner and started hammering away about the American television offer. This was not what I had dressed myself up and fought my way through the rush hour traffic for, but it did at least have the side advantage of providing me with a panoramic view of the room and the fifty or sixty people now crammed into it.

Most of them were strangers to me and to Elsa and Millie also, I suspect, for they were talking to each other in an animated fashion, which was certainly not their practice at home. Someone else must have been struck by the incongruity of it too, because as I watched, Jeremy went up to them, spoke a few words, then gripped Millie by the arm, propelled her across the room and thrust her into a group of four, who had been getting on very well without her and looked as though they could hardly wait to do so again.

This manoeuvre had left Elsa on her own, but not for long, for after a moment or two she was joined by Gregory Laycock. There was little animation now, however and, judging by his gestures and expression, he was expounding on some subject of the utmost gravity, such as the new car park. She meanwhile stood gazing up at him with the soulful look which people sometimes adopt when they can't hear, or don't want to know what it being said to them.

Perhaps my own expression was not dissimilar because at this point my agent interrupted herself to ask me what I was looking so po-faced about.

'Oh, I don't know, I just wondered if we were doing the right thing by talking shop at a gathering like this? Aren't we supposed to mingle or something?'

'Are we?' she asked, looking about her, as if for the first time. 'They appear to be getting on all right without us and I don't think I know any of these people,' which was another way of saying that none of them were clients.

'You know Ellen.'

'Yes, of course I do, my darling, but have you ever seen anyone who looks less in need of minglers?'

'Then let me take you by the hand and introduce you to some of the others. I can see one who might be glad of us.'

'Andrea's looking radiant,' I remarked, my agent having taken on Elsa, whom she could now remember having met before.

'Thank you. I like to think she always does.'

'Oh yes, but there's an extra sparkle tonight, don't you agree? But then being in love always acts like a tonic, doesn't it?'

Few more fatuous remarks can ever have been uttered, even at a gathering of this nature, because Andrea's appearance was nothing out of the ordinary and her expression sullen and discontented, while Marc, presumed to be as deeply in love as any young man alive, was comporting himself as though he had just learnt that he was to be executed at dawn.

Gregory, however, for whom flattery on this subject could not be shovelled on too lavishly, seemed oblivious of its ineptitude.

'Indeed!' he murmured, as though I had uttered a profound philosophical truth. 'Indeed, indeed! How true that is!'

146

Struggling now and thinking that even Elsa, who was no doubt being urged to persuade me to give serious thought to spending sixteen weeks in California, must be having an easier ride than mine, I tried again:

'How's her memory coming along?'

'Alas, poor child, no sign of any improvement, I fear.'

'Oh, that's too bad.'

'Yes, it is a sad blow for her, but what can one do? One can't force these things.'

'And it would probably be fatal to try, but, left to itself, it will doubtless come back after a while.'

'Evidently not,' he replied, shaking his noble head. 'It seems there is no chance of that now. We have to accept the fact that this void in her life can never be filled.'

'Oh, I wouldn't accept it yet, if I were you.'

'That is the medical verdict, on which I think perhaps I may be better qualified to speak, if you'll forgive my saying so.'

'Yes, of course I will, but I don't see how it's possible for the cleverest doctor in the world to be certain in a case like this. One day, I feel sure, some sight or sound will switch it on and everything will come back to her, as though it were yesterday.'

Evidently, he was another who liked to think that he was right and everyone else wrong, for he said:

'It would be nice to believe that, but I think you will agree that yours is a layman's view and we should not place too much reliance on it.'

I was really getting annoyed with him, both for his pomposity and his insistence on sticking to the pessimistic line, so to pay him out I said:

'A layman who speaks with experience, however,' and proceeded to relate some purely imaginary tale concerning a non-existent friend of mine, who had suffered from a similar loss of memory, only to retrieve it six months later in a train between Exeter and Newton Abbot. I must have put a lot of feeling into it too, because he listened attentively throughout

147

and by the end of it Elsa and my agent had also been halted in their tracks and become part of the audience. So I seized my chance and, by drumming up another friend, a real one this time and close at hand, was able to make my escape.

Ellen saw me to the lift.

'Thanks a lot, Tessa,' she said, while we waited for it to come up.

'What for?'

'Taking on old Greg. He's a bit heavy on hand, isn't he?'

'You could say that, and you could call him a sanctimonious old prig.'

'It's just that I can never find anything to say to him, but you were a great success. He told me you'd had a most interesting conversation.'

'It wasn't in the least interesting, it was all about his rotten, scheming little daughter.'

'Oh yes, he is obsessive about her, isn't he? Verging on the incestuous, I sometimes think. I just hope he cools down a bit once she's married. Otherwise, it seems to me that, between the two of them, Marc's life will be one long hell. What was the gist of it this evening?'

'He was going on about her amnesia and, come to think of it, Ellen, it did have its interesting side.'

'Lucky you!' she said, as the lift doors opened and I stepped inside.

'I had taken it for granted, you see, that he was worried that her memory would never come back, but I realise now that it was the other way round. I really believe he's more worried that it will.'

TWENTY-TWO

'Well, you've managed to send Alan Ferguson into a flat spin,' Robin said on Sunday morning, 'which is probably a rare achievement.'

'What about me? I'm the one who should be spinning. Imagine leaving me shut up in that loft and taking the ladder away! Do you suppose he did it on purpose?'

'No, of course not, he's drowning in remorse. Can't think what made him so stupid and careless. He puts it down to having so much on his mind and the worry about James and so forth.'

'When did he tell you all this?'

'On the telephone, while you were still asleep. He wants us to show our forgiveness by having dinner with him this evening.'

'At his bachelor quarters?'

'No, at a restaurant somewhere off Sloane Square called Chez Angelina.'

'Did you say we'd go?'

'Subject to your approval, of course. I'm to call him back, if you're otherwise engaged, or not in the mood.'

'Oh, I think we should go. It's not the sort of invitation to be turned down lightly.'

'Well, that's very magnanimous of you!'

'No, it isn't. There's something I want to ask him, and that's not all. I was taken to lunch at Angelina's when they first opened and I can tell you this, Robin, the price of our forgiveness is going to be very high indeed.'

Throughout dinner he drank only whisky and water, although this did nothing to cut down expenses, as he insisted on ordering a very superior bottle of wine for Robin and myself. As soon as this and the other preliminaries had been dealt with he started apologising for the unfortunate oversight at Orchard House and he was still at it when the smoked salmon arrived.

'Oh, please stop worrying about it,' I said for the second time. 'I'd spent a most interesting and rewarding afternoon, up to that point, so I'm not complaining.'

'It's good of you to take it so well, but I still feel guilty about it. It must have been a fearful shock and, quite honestly, I'm at a loss to know what there can have been up there to interest someone like yourself.'

'Old newspapers, for a start.'

'Old newspapers?'

'You may well sound incredulous,' Robin told him, 'but the fact is that Tessa could spend a happy afternoon reading the instructions on old detergent cartons.'

'And that's wasn't all. There were masses of photographs too.'

'Well, it takes all sorts, I suppose, but personally I'd have my work cut out to say which I'd find more tedious: old detergent cartons, or photographs of people I'd never met.'

'I had met some of them.'

'James, you mean?'

'Yes, James, of course, and yourself. There were lots of you. Not many taken when you were young, which was a pity. They were mostly quite recent, I should say.'

'Why was that a pity?'

'Because it's often instructive to see how people age, isn't it? Sometimes they develop quite differently from the way you'd expect. In your case, I'd say that , on the whole, it had been for the better.'

'Oh, thank you!'

'There were some of Rosamund too, which was also fascinating.'

'And now I know you're pulling my leg. How could you recognise, let alone be fascinated by someone whose existence you'd never heard of until after her death?'

'Easily. There were some of her and James at their wedding, so it couldn't have been anyone else. She seems to have been one of those women who changed very little as she grew older, which made it easy to pick her out in later periods. Which reminds me, Alan: there's something I've been meaning to ask you.'

'About Rosamund?' he said, without enthusiasm.

'Yes. You said, the other day, that she was attractive, or to be precise that you could understand men finding her attractive.'

'Did I? Well, yes, I daresay I may have said something of the kind.'

'Then I hope you won't mind my asking, but did that imply that you found her attractive yourself?'

'Me? Good heavens, no, not in that sense. She was my wife's cousin, part of the family.'

'All the same, there must have been some basis for your remark. So, if you personally never thought of her in that way, presumably you knew of at least one man who did? How else could she have given you that impression?'

'I know of one who did, certainly.'

'One will do.'

'I doubt that, because I am referring to her husband. He was very much in love with her.'

'But how do you reconcile that with . . . ?' I began, but Robin who had taken no part in the conversation, had now listened to enough of it:

'Leave the poor man alone, Tessa! He hasn't brought us out to dinner to be cross-examined. Let's talk about something else. Like this excellent wine, for instance.'

We talked about the excellent wine and a number of other topics and the subject of Rosamund was not referred to again, but I doubt if she was forgotten. I twice caught Alan glancing at me and I could tell from his expression that he had guessed what I had been about to say when Robin headed me off. He continued to be friendly on the surface, but there was an awkwardness and uncertainty in his

151

manner which had not been there before and it was evident from the way he sometimes lost track of the conversation that part of his mind had travelled a long way off. He gave the impression of a man who, had there been a loft handy, would have been happy to have shut me up in it.

So, by and large, an unrewarding evening for all three of us, the only people to gain being the management and staff of Chez Angelina.

Later that night Andrea made a half-hearted attempt to commit suicide. Whether she had genuinely intended it to succeed is wide open to question, but if so she had soon changed her mind.

She was spending the night in London, in order to keep an early appointment on Monday with her dressmaker and, within seconds of swallowing the last of three or four dozen seasick pills, had picked up the telephone to call Ellen, who had risen to the occasion with her usual aplomb.

Nevertheless, I found it astonishing that, in an emergency of this nature, Andrea should have appealed to someone she had only known for a few weeks.

'Perhaps that was the reason, Tess. Or perhaps she is beginning to look on me as the mother figure her life has always lacked. The fact that I'm younger than she is wouldn't interfere with that.'

'And of course you do manage to exude a blend of tranquillity and common sense, which attracts parasites like Andrea. On the other hand, one thing her life has never lacked is a father figure. But he was in the country, presumably?'

'It wouldn't have made any difference if he'd been in the house next door. She's scared stiff he'll find out. It was about midnight when Jeremy and I got there. She was still conscious and, luckily, she'd done as I told her and unlocked the front door. So he carried her down to the car and we drove to the nearest Casualty. She was pretty dopey by then, but she kept saying over and over again that I must promise not to tell her father.'

'He's bound to find out, though, isn't he? She'll most likely tell him herself when she's wrung the last drop from this drama and needs to set up a new one.'

'Maybe, but I doubt it, somehow. I don't think it was an act this time.'

'What happened when you got to the hospital?'

'We had to hang about for over an hour, which was pretty rough on Jeremy, who has to get up in the morning. Then one of the doctors came out and told us she was going to be okay, but they were keeping her in for the night, so we were able to pack it in and go home.'

'And what about Marc? Is he not to be told either?'

'No, although she didn't warn me about that until this morning, when I went round to the hospital to take her some clothes and a toothbrush and so on. She doesn't want to see him, either, not yet, anyway. It presents itself as a somewhat dodgy problem, but we think we've worked out a scheme to keep him at bay for a few days.'

'You don't happen to know why she tried to kill herself, by any chance?'

'No, she didn't tell me and I didn't ask. I thought you might want to, though.'

'I wouldn't half mind, but I can't, at this moment, see how it's to be done.'

'Well, here's what we're going to do, Tessa. They're turfing her out of the hospital this afternoon and she'll be coming to us for a day or two. It was the only thing to do. She's in no state to be on her own at the flat and she can't go home to Daddy either, looking as she does. So we'll take care of that by making sure she rings him up for a chat every evening.'

'And how about Marc? Did you say you had a plan for him too?'

'Yes. He was a much worse problem, naturally, but we've fudged up a story about how she's staying with us for a few days because she's got an infection.'

'And he'll be round to call, with the champagne and roses before you can count to ten.'

'No, he won't,' Ellen said. 'The champagne and roses may arrive, but he won't be with them. What she has, you see, is a slight temperature and swollen glands and the doctor says it may easily turn out to be mumps. That was Jeremy's brilliant idea. He rang up Marc and said "Listen, old boy, have you ever had the mumps?" and got the right answer. We're hoping of course that in a day or two Andrea will have a change of heart and decide to stay alive and get married. Then it'll turn out not to be mumps, after all, but that's the situation at present.'

'And it does seem to cover all eventualities. Congratulations!'

'I hope you'll approve of the next bit too. Jeremy and I are supposed to be dining with his parents tonight, but I don't want to come home and find Andrea's cleaned us out of aspirin, so he'll go on his own. I wondered if you'd care to come and have an invalid supper and keep us company? That is, if Robin wouldn't mind being left out? I don't envisage it as exactly his sort of evening.'

'I don't think he'll mind at all,' I assured her. 'I'm pretty certain he hasn't had mumps either.'

In saying that Ellen had covered all eventualities, I had underestimated Gregory Laycock. It was a little after half-past seven and we were sitting in Andrea's bedroom when the doorbell rang and Ellen went to answer it. She was gone for a full ten minutes, the first part of which I spent trying, without success, to get some response out of the patient. She refused to be drawn on any of the topics I tried on her, finally informing me that she did not feel well enough to talk. It must be said that she did not look at all well, but I did not believe this was the true cause of her distaste for conversation. I had the impression that she was straining both ears to catch some sound from outside the room and this was confirmed when she broke the silence at last by saying, in the

154

tinniest of voices:

'Who on earth do you suppose would be calling at this time of night?'

'I really couldn't tell you.'

'Perhaps, if you were to open the door, you'd hear something?'

'Oh, very well,' I said, getting up and doing so. Looking down the passage, I saw that the sitting-room door was the only one of the four within view which was closed.

'Not a sound,' I reported, re-entering the bedroom and shutting the door behind me.

'What do you suppose it can mean?'

'Who knows? Perhaps whoever it was has gone now and Ellen's in the kitchen knocking up the dinner.'

'Why don't you go and see?'

I was searching for a way out of this when Ellen saved me the trouble.

'It's your father,' she told Andrea, who banged her head back against the pillow and closed her eyes.

'I don't want to see him. Tell him to go away.'

'He refuses to go away.'

'Tell him I'm not feeling well.'

'I have told him, several times. He says all the more reason why he should see you and make sure you're getting proper attention.'

'How did he know I was here? Did Marc tell him?'

'Yes, but you can't blame him for that. It seems that you didn't put on a very convincing act when you telephoned home this afternoon. Your father smelt a battalion of rats and came hurtling up to London to find out what was going on. When he discovered that you weren't at the flat and your bedroom was in a shocking mess he became more worried than ever and he got hold of Marc. It was something we hadn't allowed for, but, since we're now stuck with it, surely you could give him just a few minutes, Andrea? Then you can tell him you're feeling better and you'll be home in a day or two. I'm sure that's all he wants.'

'No, it's not all he wants,' Andrea said, her voice rising to a squeak, 'and I won't see him, I won't.'

Even the resourceful Ellen was nonplussed and she turned to me with a helpless expression.

'What to do, Tessa?'

'You and Jeremy could move into an hotel, I suppose. Apart from that, I see no easy solution. Any good my having a go at trying to dislodge him?'

'Why not? It couldn't do any harm.'

'You'd never know with this lot,' I said, 'whether it could or it couldn't, but I'll do my best.'

'Andrea sends her love and wishes you to know that she is being well looked after. She is a little tired, though and not in the mood for visitors. Have you time for a drink before you leave?'

'I don't want a drink, thank you and I have no intention of leaving until I have seen my daughter.'

'Then I shall have one, while we sit out the first couple of hours,' I said, helping myself. 'Fortunately, this flat runs to two spare bedrooms. That's the lovely thing about having a lot of money, I always say. It brings these fringe benefits, as well as the calculable ones. Now, what shall we talk about? Or would you prefer a game of cards? That might pass the time even better.'

I had decided, the instant I entered the room and saw him sitting stiffly upright, like a martyred saint and wearing the expression of one who had the strength of ten, that ridicule, rather than argument, should be my weapon. So I kept it up for another four or five minutes, by which time I had been rewarded by signs that he was beginning to crack. He still looked noble and aggrieved, but an understandable weariness was creeping in and I estimated that the strength had now shrunk to something nearer to that of six or seven.

'And how are things at Sowerley?' I asked. 'Have you seen Elsa lately? I feel sure you have. You and she must have endless matters to discuss about plans for the wedding.

156

My goodness, what a worry for you both! I daresay you'll be relieved when it's over. I know Millie will. She tells me she is not at all looking forward to being a bridesmaid and she . . .'

Goaded beyond endurance, Gregory raised his hand, in a request for silence, which I was happy to comply with.

'I realise that you find all this vastly amusing, Mrs Price . . .'

'Oh, do call me Tessa!'

'Tessa, then. You may find it amusing, but I assure you that I do not. The situation is extremely distasteful to me.'

'Yes, it must be. Not only distasteful, but a shade frustrating, I should imagine?'

'It is worse than that. I shall go now, but you may tell Ellen that I do not intend to let the matter rest. I shall consult my solicitor in the morning. In my view, this is tantamount to coercion.'

'It is nothing of the kind and your solicitor will die laughing. Andrea is here at her own wish, staying with friends. She doesn't happen to want to see you at the moment, but she's twenty-six and that's her business.'

'We shall see,' he replied, gathering up the tattered remnants of his dignity. 'Please don't get up, I can see myself out.'

Nevertheless, I accompanied him all the way to the front door, less out of courtesy than to ensure that he did not turn in the wrong direction.

'The coast is now clear,' I announced, returning to the bedroom.

'Oh, well done! You're a genius, Tess! And now I can go and do something about the dinner. You stay here and talk to Andrea.'

'So tell me what it's all about?' I said, seating myself in the armchair which Ellen had just vacated. 'Why did you want to kill yourself and why are you so petrified of your father? Or is the answer the same to both questions?'

'Why don't you mind your own business?'

'It has become my business,' I told her, 'after what I have just been through on your behalf. You can't expect oceans of co-operation without giving a drop or two in return. Still more is it Ellen's business, since you have chosen to lumber her with your presence and all that it entails. She has too much delicacy to question you herself, so you will have to put up with it from me.'

'What happens if I refuse to answer?'

'I'll tell you exactly what happens. You'll end up in a worse jam than you're in already. You can't spend the rest of your life as a suspected mumps case, any more than you can spend it skulking in this flat. Sooner or later you'll have to stand up and deal with the problem, so you may as well get into practice by starting on me. You never know, I might even be able to help.'

'No one can help me,' she moaned, with a despairing and dramatic flop against the pillows.

Watching her, I said: 'And, incidentally, Andrea, there's one other question I forgot to ask. Why have you been trying to con everyone into believing that you've lost your memory? Or is the answer the same there, as well?'

She came out of her corner again, on her toes, fists flying:

'What do you mean? How dare you say such a thing? I haven't been trying to con anyone about anything. I did lose my memory and it hasn't come back. The doctors say . . .'

'Oh, don't give me that all over again, I implore you! You can tell me till you're blue in the face what the doctors say and I shan't believe a word of it. It's a preposterous story and you'd never have got away with it, without expert co-operation, from your father this time. He backed you up, either to save your face, or for reasons of his own and, being a doctor himself, his word carried weight, so most people accepted it. I suppose it was connected with what happended when your house caught fire?'

It was like taking a rattle from a sleeping baby. She stared at me with an appalled expression, which wasn't put on this time, and said:

'You mean, you know about that? Does everyone know?'

'I don't know anything, I was hoping you'd tell me. Did you start it yourself, by any chance?'

'No, of course not. How can you sit there, saying these horrible things? Of course I didn't start it myself.'

'How do you know?'

'How do I . . . I just do, that's all.'

'I don't see how you can be sure. Your memory gap is supposed to start at the point where you were saying goodnight to Marc outside a cinema. After that, you tell us, everything has been wiped out. So how do you know you didn't go home, empty a gin bottle over your step-mother's eiderdown and set fire to it?'

'What gin bottle . . . ? . . . I mean, I couldn't have. It's just not the sort of thing I'd ever do.'

'Admittedly, it's not the sort of thing many people would enjoy remembering about themselves, so if that's what you did it's no wonder you're going to such lengths to forget it.'

'I didn't, I tell you. I didn't, I didn't, I know I didn't. Oh, do leave me alone, can't you?'

'Okay, I'll lay off now, but if I were you I'd give it some thought. You don't seem to be very happy on the path you're treading now, so you might do better to face reality, instead of trying to push it out of your mind.'

I did not add that, if she were to heed this advice, she would know whom to confide in, because I did not believe there was much chance that she would. All the same, my bullying had not been quite in vain, since I had at least proved, to my own satisfaction at any rate, that there had been something fishy about the fire.

There was also the pleasure of knowing that, to this extent, I had been right and Toby wrong, and when I got home I was tempted to ring him up and tell him so.

I refrained, however, partly from fear of his pointing out that it did nothing whatever to exculpate James McGrath, and partly because I needed all my wits and faculties to work out a theory whereby it could be made to do so.

TWENTY-THREE

The photographic memory came in handy because there were two Alan Fergusons in the telephone directory, but no Isobel. There were also numerous A's and I's and it was only the recollection of the address at the top of her letter to Elsa that guided me to the number I wanted.

Thanks to my excavations in the loft, I could picture her appearance too, and the voice fitted the personality I had endowed her with; not coy, but definitely uncertain and hard to please.

All this, naturally, gave me the advantage and when I said that, having just returned from sixteen weeks in Los Angeles and heard the shattering news about her cousin, who had been a friend of mine, and wondered whether I might call on her, she seemed at a loss for a suitable way to refuse.

'I don't know, Mrs . . . I'm sorry, I didn't quite catch your name.'

'Price, but my professional name is Theresa Crichton.'

'Oh, good heavens! I thought your voice was somehow familiar, but I had no idea Rosamund even knew you.'

'Well, it must be over a year now since we met, but I used to see a lot of her when I was staying with my aunt in Sussex.'

'But how strange that she never mentioned you!'

'It is rather, because I feel I know an awful lot about you and your two daughters and Alan, your husband, of course. But then, she was a bit like that in some ways, wasn't she?'

'Was she? Like what? I'm not sure I understand.'

'Oh, you know, sort of keeping her life in separate compartments.'

'Yes, that's true, I suppose. All the same . . . '

'I also got the impression that you were a great theatre buff.'

160

'That's certainly true.'

'It's mainly what gave me the nerve to ring you up. I'd really awfully like to meet you, if you could put up with me for half an hour.'

'Well, it's very kind of you to say so. I don't know. When would you like to come?'

'Right now, if I may? I've been lunching round the corner from where you live, you see.'

'Oh well, in that case . . . yes, come and have a cup of tea.'

The sitting-room was muted and in every way unremarkable, except for its spotlessness. Not the sort of room where one could imagine anyone sprawling about and dropping newspapers on the floor, and there wasn't an ashtray in sight.

The owner was cut to the same aseptic pattern. She gave the impression that no single hair was ever out of place, even when she woke up in the morning, one could picture her wiping the sausages before putting them in the frying pan, and her clothes looked as though they were being worn for the first time.

'I'd like to make it clear,' I said, accepting my tea, which was very weak and served in a fragile little cup, so designed as to ensure that it would instantly become tepid as well, 'that I've no wish to probe into the circumstances of Rosamund's death, or even discuss it, if you'd rather not, but sometimes people can be overtactful, don't you find? They are so determined not to intrude that they shy off the subject altogether and you're not allowed to talk about it, even if you want to.'

Her hand trembled as she put her cup down and tears flooded her pale, protruberant blue eyes.

'You know, it's extraordinary you should say that. You must be the first person to understand what I've been through during these past two weeks. Even my daughters change the subject when I mention it. As though they found it not so much sad and shocking as downright embarrassing.'

'Yes, I can understand that.'

'Can you really? Personally, I find their attitude quite incomprehensible. I don't mean that I want to talk about it all the time, but naturally one thinks of very little else and it seems so unnatural to try and hide it away and pretend it hasn't happened. Some of my friends are even worse. They make me feel like a pariah, As though I was the one who had committed some unmentionable crime.'

'They're so afraid of saying the wrong thing that they daren't risk saying anything at all.'

'Well, I call that selfish and unkind. They ought to consider my feelings a bit more. Even the wrong thing would be preferable to being ostracised. You'll hardly believe this, but the other day a woman I've known for years literally crossed over to the other side of the road when she saw me coming. She pretended to be looking in a shop window, but I know it was really to avoid me. I expect you think I'm exaggerating, but I assure you I'm not and I'm really grateful for the chance to unburden myself. I was a bit knocked off my perch when you suggested coming, but I'm glad now that you did. It was very kind and thoughtful of you.'

It was a pleasure to hear this for several reasons, not least in that I saw it as partially excusing the trick I had played on her and, seizing the chance to keep the unburdening rolling along, I said:

'Well, I expect that being Rosamund's friend and not yours makes it easier for me to be detached, as well as sympathetic. I might not have behaved any better than the people you've been talking about, if something terrible like this had happened to you, but at least I'd have known how she felt. There was a great bond between you two, wasn't there? You were more like sisters than cousins, I believe?'

'Yes, that used to be so. I was a few years older than her, but we were inseparable when we were young and even our marriages didn't seem to interfere with that. We still saw a

162

lot of each other, on our own and sometimes the four of us together, and we used to talk endlessly on the telephone. Somehow or other, things hadn't been quite the same for the past year or two. No quarrel, but just a gradual falling off.'

'Yes, that's the impression I had and I wondered about it. I thought there might have been some coolness on your side, but it seems I was wrong. What do you suppose can have made her turn against you?'

'Oh, I wouldn't put it as strongly as that. We were still outwardly the same whenever we did meet, it was just that the meetings became so much more spaced out. It was always I who rang up and suggested one and she invariably had some reason why she couldn't manage it. I can't remember how or when it all started, I just suddenly woke up one morning and realised that I hadn't heard from her for over three months.'

'But you couldn't think of any reason?'

'None at all. Looking back on it, I think the first signs of a change in her attitude must have coincided with their selling the house in Sussex and moving to Oxfordshire. I suppose I just assumed that she was completely taken up with that and everything would get back to normal once she and James had settled in. It never did, though.'

'I don't know about you, Mrs Ferguson, but to me that makes it all the more puzzling. I'd have thought being separated from all her old friends would have made her more dependent on you, not less.'

'It is strange, isn't it? You met James, of course?'

'Yes, I did, several times.'

'At first, I tried to make excuses for her by telling myself that he was to blame, but I don't think I believed it, even then. Why should he suddenly take it into his head to drive a wedge between us, after all these years? It's true that I never much cared for him and, whether he murdered my poor Rosamund or not, I do think he often treated her abominably. But I was careful not to criticise him openly.'

'So there must have been some other reason?'

'There must, and now I shall never know what it was or what I was supposed to have done to annoy her. It worries me a lot. Of course, knowing wouldn't alter anything, but not knowing does somehow make it worse. I wonder if you can understand?'

'Yes, I can, but I think it's a mistake to put all the blame on yourself.'

'That's the way I'm made, I'm afraid. I've had some hard knocks in my life, nothing to compare with this, naturally, but they seemed bad enough at the time and with each one I've felt that, in some way I can't account for, I must have brought it on myself.'

'Well, since this is the worst thing that's ever happened, or is ever likely to happen, it might be the time to shake yourself out of that attitude. Much as I liked her, it sounds to me as though it was Rosamund who was at fault and that you should stop reproaching yourself.'

'It would be some comfort to believe that, but I must have done something wrong, to make her wish to avoid me.'

'Not necessarily. I should say it was more likely that she had done something which she believed would annoy or offend you.'

'Oh no, I can't think of anything which would do that, I really can't.'

'Not if she was having an affair with some man she had good reason to believe you wouldn't approve of?'

'I might not have approved, but I would never have condemned her for it. For one thing, James was often unfaithful to her and she knew it. I think she excused it on the grounds that having no children gave him the right to be more irresponsible as a husband. I admit it did once cross my mind that there might have been some tit for tat going on, but I soon dismissed that idea.'

'Why?'

'Mainly, I think, because of my husband's reaction when I suggested it to him. You may have heard that he and I are separated now, but in those days . . . Well, I suppose it was

164

at about the same time as things started to go wrong between me and Alan, which made me feel more cut off than ever. I needed so badly to talk to Rosamund and put my side of it to her. Anyway, to get back to what I was saying, I forget what arguments Alan used, but they were very convincing. He and I may have become incompatible in other ways, but I had great respect for his judgement and I still have. He is able to see things more clearly than I do.'

'Well, since you've ruled out that possibility, let's try to think 'of some other reason she might have had for her behaviour.'

'But I promise you I can't think of anything, Miss Crichton. Can you?'

'No. That is . . . unless . . . you'll probably tell me I'm all at sea here, but I suppose it couldn't have anything to do with her plan to adopt a child?'

'Oh, she told you about that, did she?'

'There was some mention of it and it occurred to me that she'd discussed it with you and you'd been against it. If she'd intended to go ahead anyway, and ignore your advice, she might have chosen to keep away, rather than get into arguments about it.'

'Oh, no, no, there wouldn't have been any arguments from me. I was all for it.'

'Oh, I see! So that's out too, then?'

'The arguments had all been the other way round. My only complaint was that she'd left it so late.'

'I suppose she put it off, so long as there was a chance that she would have a child of her own?'

'Oh, but didn't she tell you . . . ? Well no, it obviously wasn't the sort of thing one would discuss with anyone outside the family, but the truth is that she never intended to have any children. It was quite deliberate and she made it clear to James before they married. I don't think it bothered him, one way or the other.'

'Was she frightened of childbirth?'

'No, nothing like that, but when she was very young she

165

suffered from the most crippling asthma. She grew out of it eventually, but it made life a misery for her throughout her childhood and when she was sixteen she very nearly died. That was partly what made us so close. I could recognise the symptoms when an attack was coming on and I used to try and protect her and help her through them. Just watching her was agony and when she was still in her teens she swore that, whatever happened, she would never risk passing it on to a child of her own.'

'But the attacks had ceased by the time she married?'

'Pretty well, but that didn't alter her determination never to have a child. Let me give you some more tea?'

'No thanks, I think it's time I went home. I'm sorry I haven't been much help.'

'Oh, don't say that! It's been a relief just having someone to talk to and I feel better for it. I hope we can meet again, when this dreadful business is over.'

'I hope so too and I'll send you some tickets for my next play, touching wood that there'll be one.'

'How kind! Is it likely to be soon?'

I was on the point of explaining that immediate plans included the probability of sixteen weeks in Los Angeles, but recollected myself in time and, by way of reply, held up both hands, with fingers crossed.

'I have found another link,' I announced to Toby, who was spending the night with us at Beacon Square, 'maybe one and a half.'

He had been induced to make one of his rare visits to London by the need to turn an honest penny and had spent the afternoon in conference with his agent and a West End manager, who was showing stirrings of interest in the current, half completed T. Crichton comedy.

'Keep it up and you will soon have a whole chain. Whose neck do you propose to use it as a noose for?'

'I haven't got to that stage yet, nor even made up my mind whether, after all, there are two separate chains, which don't

166

join at any point. All the same, I feel I am piecing something together. How would it be if I were to try it out on you?'

'It would be all right, I suppose, but I should warn you that I am not at my most alert. It has been an exhausting session.'

'And I should warn you that I am about to demolish your theory that Andrea spent her lost weekend with James at the cottage.'

'You have evidence to prove that she was elsewhere?'

'Not exactly, no. Only to indicate that she was not in Wales.'

'That may do just as well. I'll let you know when I've heard it.'

'There are two factors which, in my opinion, rule it out. The first, which has been with us from the beginning, is that if she and James had planned an adventure of that sort, it could not have been a last minute arrangement. They would have worked out the moves in advance and, knowing her father as she does, the first requirement would have been to set up a convincing alibi for him. She would need someone to rely on to back her up in whatever lies she had told him about where and with whom she would be staying. The Hebrideans were ideally suited for this role. In the event of Gregory getting steamed up about his baby girl, as indeed he did, they had only to say that she was fine, but unfortunately had twisted her ankle while tramping over the glens and was unable to get to the telephone. However, as we know, they did nothing of the kind.'

'Perhaps, when it came to the point, they betrayed her? Didn't want to take the responsibility?'

'Oh, come on, Toby, that's pretty feeble. She's twenty-six, not sixteen. Their only responsibility would have been a couple of lies on their conscience and most people can tolerate that, if they're doing it for a friend.'

'Nevertheless, I hope you have something a shade more weighty than that for your demolition?'

'I shall now tell you,' I said, 'of a conversation which I had with our heroine on her sickbed yesterday evening,' and, having done so, added:

'So far as I am concerned, that is enough to show that the pretence of amnesia was not put on to disguise her failure to account for her movements. It was the other way round. Her failure to account for her movements was the build-up to convince people that she had lost her memory.'

'Is there a difference?'

'Of course there is. It must mean that she either saw, heard, or did something connected with the fire, which she now wishes to forget.'

'And in the meantime James continues to languish in gaol. I don't see what you have to be so cocky about?'

'I expected you to take that attitude and I admit you have cause, but the point is that we are clearing the decks. Now that we can safely assume that he and Andrea did not spend that weekend together, we have at least removed one complication.'

'Which is bad news for you, because the more complications you remove, the more certainly you're left with the bare bones of the case against him.'

'You could be right and, if so, I'll have to give up and admit that I was taken in by flattery and all those other things you accused me of, but I'm not ready to do that yet. You remember my telling you that I had also found half a link? Well, this afternoon I had tea with a woman called Isobel Ferguson, who is Rosamund McGrath's cousin, and she had some interesting facts to relate concerning her ex-husband. It is hard to believe that he could have had any hand in setting fire to Mrs Laycock's bedroom, but it does begin to look as though he knows rather more about the life, and possibly death of Rosamund McGrath than he has seen fit to disclose. And that is what matters to us, is it not?'

'Speak for yourself! I cannot honestly say that it matters to me. What interesting facts?' Toby asked, contradicting himself in the same breath.

'One was that he refused to entertain the idea that she had a lover. Isobel could not remember what argument he had used, only that they were very convincing and, because she has become conditioned to regarding his opinions as divinely inspired, she accepted this one, without question. However, I do not.'

'Why?'

'Well, I ask you, Toby, how could any man make a judgement of that kind about any woman? Those very convincing arguments become even more absurd in the light of another comment he made about Rosamund, which was that she was attractive. As a matter of fact, he regretted having said that when I reminded him of it later, but I know he meant it at the time. So why the hell shouldn't she have had a lover? James knew she had and claims that she made no secret of it.'

'Oh, I expect this Ferguson was bored to tears by his wife going on about it and simply wanted to shut her up.'

'Maybe, but that wasn't the only way he betrayed himself. When James was arrested Alan told me that, much as he deplored it, he was unable to see any alternative to his being guilty. Then a few days later, to settle another argument, he calmly announces that James was very much in love with Rosamund. Well, funny way of showing it, is all I can say. You know, Toby, I am beginning to believe that shutting me in the loft wasn't just absent-mindedness. I was making him nervous with all my questions and he had this subconscious desire to shut me up, in the abstract sense. So, when the chance came, he did it literally.'

'I can sympathise with him there, but I agree that he should not have let his subconscious run away with him. So what's his game and what is he nervous about?'

'Well, let's say, for example, that he killed Rosamund and would like someone else to take the blame for it.'

'I suppose, in his shoes, we all would, but it's a biggish jump isn't it?'

'Not if we accept the premise that he was her lover.'

'And are we ready to accept it?'

'Why not? He seems to fit all the requirements.'

'Simply by virtue of saying one day that she couldn't have had one and the next that he found her attractive? It is damning, I agree, but not conclusive, surely?'

'Oh, he has tangled himself up in more ways than that. Like all inarticulate people, when he turns garrulous he doesn't know where to stop. For instance, when James was arrested and Alan started trying to convince me of his guilt, he assured me that there was no truth in the rumour about Rosamund's infidelities, which had been going around after her disappearance. That struck me as odd at the time because how could he have known about them, except from the inside? He hadn't been back to Sowerley then and they certainly hadn't been passed on to him by Isobel. That was his first mistake and he made another when I kept nagging him about James's motive. He suggested that it was linked with her inability to have children. Well, that was a falsification, to start with, as I now know, but he went further. He piled on a few more bricks by quoting from his own experience.'

'What was that?'

'Asking Isobel for a divorce, so that he could marry someone else, which she refused to grant him. He described how this had created a certain amount of bitterness and resentment, which in different circumstances, i.e. childlessness, might conceivably have turned his own thoughts to murder. So far, so good, but instead of leaving it there he had to go on and tell us to within a month or two when this happened, and that's what I meant about not knowing where to stop.'

'Why?'

'Because it coincided almost exactly with Rosamund's abortive attempt to leave James. So, if Alan had been the man she was leaving him for, wouldn't that explain everything? She and Alan have decided to run away and, as the first step along this path, Rosamund packs her bags and moves out, leaving a note to James to say that she will not be returning. However, the second step is never taken because

Isobel refuses to co-operate. Faced with this impasse, they adjust accordingly. Alan is now the one to move out, whereas Rosamund goes back to James, but this is not the end of it. They have reverted to their former positions, but with the difference that they now have the privacy and opportunity to meet and carry on their affair whenever she can find an excuse to spend a few days away from home. What do you think of the story, so far?'

'Not bad, but too circumstantial. The fact that the two marriages came unstuck at about the same time doesn't prove there was a connection.'

'Someone said that proof can sometimes mean lack of imagination and there is plenty of evidence to suggest one.'

'What evidence?'

'The rift between Rosamund and Isobel, which also started at that time. Isobel could find no way to account for it, but I can. If my reconstruction is right, she'd have been the last person Rosamund would have confided in. Therefore, being unable to do so, she preferred to have no communication with her at all. How does that strike you?'

'With a resounding clatter, although it still does not show Alan to be the murderer.'

'You say that because you haven't heard the best bit yet. I have been saving it till the end.'

'And the right place for it, I always say. Not bad, either, to know that the end is approaching. What is the best bit?'

'It hinges on the muddle over that trip to Wales. It's obvious that James was expecting Alan to join him. Why else would he have laid in extra stocks of food and made up two beds? Obviously, also, Alan could not deny that the arrangement had existed, having doubtless mentioned it to various other people. So he plays it down, pretends it was only a loose arrangement and, hearing no more about it, concluded the trip was off. However, it's my belief that he had every intention of going and only changed his mind at the last minute. And why was that, you ask?'

'Oh, do I?'

171

'Yes, and I shall tell you. On Thursday night, the eve of his departure, he listened to the nine o'clock news. Just in case you need to be reminded, that was when we first heard about the missing boy. By Friday morning, when Alan was due to leave, a full-scale search was under way. That was why he changed his mind. It had been his intention all along that James should be arrested for Rosamund's murder, but he had no desire to be with him when it happened.'

'My dear Tessa, you amaze me sometimes! I had never expected to accuse you of underestimating yourself, but you have done it now. It is not half a link, it is practically the clasp to fasten the chain. All you need to do now is to find out why he killed her and the battle's won.'

'Yes', I admitted with a sigh, 'as someone is said to have remarked in another context, there's the rub!'

TWENTY-FOUR

The christening was to take place on the following Saturday, and Friday morning had been set aside for buying a hat in which to grace this occasion, and also a present for my month-old godson.

I had asked Ellen if she would help me to choose them, which she had agreed to do, on condition that Andrea could tag along. 'She's almost on her feet now,' she explained, 'but we don't want any slipping back and, the more mental therapy we can lay on, the sooner we'll be able to launch her on to the world again. Buying hats should be just the job. All those mirrors!'

We met on the second floor of a giant department store and I soon saw the wisdom of the words, for Andrea was in her element. She tried on every hat that was brought up for my inspection, wandered up and down the showroom, admiring her reflection from all angles, monopolised the saleswoman and generally showed more animation and good humour than at any time during our acquaintance.

'It's a mystery to me,' I remarked to Ellen, while we waited for the box containing the white panama which was supposed to go with everything, 'how any normal-sized hat could fit that head.'

'It is puffed-out with vanity,' she explained, 'and that brings it up to average dimensions.'

'Well, another couple of hours of this and she'd be ready to take on all the fathers and fiancés the world has to offer. Let's hope she'll find something to adore among the cuddly toys.'

'You're not going for a silver mug, then?'

'No, he's only four weeks old, so what could he do with it? And his mother, who ought to know, tells me he would prefer a pram cover. I shall throw in a teddy to make it more personalised, and Andrea can help me choose him. That should make her happy.'

It was among the more inaccurate forecasts, however, because as soon as we entered the Toys and Babycare Department the mood changed and it became clear that we were heading for trouble.

It covered an area of several acres and was stuffed with enough merchandise from prams, cots and paddling pools, down to size one bootees, to satisfy the needs and gladden the hearts of several thousand children, about half of whom appeared to have turned up to test the truth of this.

The immediate effect of this sea of plenty, on myself at any rate, was quite dizzying, but Ellen was able to guide us unerringly to the layette section. It consisted of a single counter, running the entire length of the room, with shelves behind it and a row of chairs in front, which she instantly realised had been placed there for the comfort and convenience of the expectant-mother consumers. It was while we were moving in single file towards it that things started to go wrong.

Ellen led the way, followed at a distance by Andrea, whose mind must still have been up with the hats on the floor above because, for no discernible reason, she became involved in a traffic incident.

It occurred at the intersection of two aisles. Coming towards us, on our own, was a woman dragging a small child by the hand, while at right angles to us a boy of about five was hurtling along on an erratic course in the wake of an outsize doll's pram, whose handlebar was on a level with his eyes. The other woman stopped to let him pass, but Andrea did not. She walked straight into the pram, which lurched sideways, causing the boy to lose his grasp and fall over, and striking terror into the hearts of the other child and its mother. Both children instantly began bawling at the top of their lungs, which brought about half a dozen other people running in, to add to the turmoil. In the gradual sorting out which ensued, Andrea, whose leg was bleeding, stood white-faced and silent with a dazed expression on her face, as though unable to comprehend what was happening or what had caused it.

There was one vacant chair beside the counter, so I offered it to her whose need seemed greatest. No gesture could have been more ill-conceived, though, and the climax we had been working up to now swept over us like a gust of wind heralding a storm.

Andrea's face, which had been so pale, puckered and changed to scarlet. She clenched her fists, banged them on the counter and began to scream. She went on screaming until Ellen gave her two resounding slaps across the face and then, after a moment's silence, subsided, whimpering, into the chair.

It had now become my turn to stand transfixed, taking no part in the action, but asking myself how I could have been so blind. So many links and chains were clinking around in my head that I forgot all about the white panama and followed the other two, first to the Ladies' Rest Room and then into a taxi, in a state of semi-trance. The only thought I could keep a firm hold on was that I was at last beginning to understand what it was that Andrea had been trying so hard to forget.

Admittedly, at this stage it was partly guesswork, but belief that I was right and everyone else wrong had never been stronger. It made me determined to press on and find some evidence to support it, however hard the going might be. That it would be hard was plain from the outset, because there were questions to be answered by a number of people, not all of whom were necessarily disposed to co-operate, which always calls for a modicum of diplomacy, and there were worse obstacles than that to contend with here. In moments of low ebb they appeared almost insuperable, since of the half-dozen or so whose knowledge I most needed to draw on, two were scarcely on speaking terms with me, one was in police custody and two were dead.

Luckily, there remained one who suffered from none of these disadvantages and during dinner that evening I asked Robin whether there was any chance of my being allowed to visit James McGrath.

'The short answer is no,' he replied.

'Not even for five minutes?'

'Not even for one. Why do you want to?'

'I have a couple of questions for him.'

'You don't give up, do you?'

'Why should I, when I really believe I'm on to something at last? Besides, you've told me more than once that you're not convinced he's guilty.'

'In which case, he'll be acquitted, presumably.'

'I'd rather make certain of it.'

'What makes you think he'd be willing to answer your questions?'

'The fact that they have no direct bearing on the murder. Or rather, not in a way to implicate him. It concerns a matter of adoption. I want to know whether he and Rosamund were planning to adopt a child at the time of her death and, if so, what stage the negotiations had reached.'

'And supposing the answer should be no, they were not planning anything of the kind?'

'Then I should bow out gracefully, because that is what I regard as the cornerstone of my theory. Everything else stands or falls by it.'

'Then write a letter and I'll do my best to see that it gets to him through his solicitor. That's the most I can promise.'

'Thank you, Robin, that'll do nicely. And now see what you can do with this one!'

'Oh, not another! Does it never strike you that I have any work of my own to bother about?'

'This is only a trifle, but it needs a voice of authority to bring quick results. It would probably take me about six weeks, if I were to try to do it on my own.'

'Oh, very well, give me the worst!'

'It concerns a birth certificate. I can't be precise over

176

details, only the year and the month, but I expect what will be enough.'

'Then you had better make a note of it, such as it is.'

When I had done so and handed it to him, he looked up, frowning:

'Are you sure about this Tessa?'

'My information comes from a reliable source.'

'And it really has some bearing on the McGrath case?'

'Oh yes, it concerns him as much as anyone.'

'All right, I'll do what I can. Nothing else you need, I suppose, while I'm about it?'

'Well, there is just one other tiny thing, as it happens.'

'Oh, God! Why did I speak?'

'This is personal. I was thinking that perhaps we ought to invite Alan here one evening? We do owe him a dinner, you know.'

'Yes, we do, but I'm not at all sure that he'll come. I'm even less sure that I want him to. Not after all that probing and pestering that went on last time the three of us had dinner together.'

'Well, you won't have to put up with it this time. Invite him for seven-thirty and then make sure that you have to work late that evening. Ten minutes is all I need.'

'It may be more than you'll get. I still doubt if he'll want to come.'

'Probably not,' I agreed. 'I'm pinning my hopes on the hunch that he'll find it harder to stay away.'

Having started these wheels turning, the next job was to put a call through to Sowerley Grange. Elsa had told me that the secretarial college was now closed for the summer and that she was finding it a bit of a trial having Millie at home all day. She would be going to Brittany with some friends in July, but for the time being could find nothing better to do than grumble incessantly about the iniquity of throwing all that money away on a boring old wedding, when half the world was starving. So I had devised a small holiday task for

177

her, to take her mind off things.

'I think you should try your hand at a crime story,' I told her. 'Not a fictional one, exactly, because you won't have to invent anything. It's all there for the taking. Just think of it Millie! How many budding journalists are lucky enough to have a real-life murder right on their doorstep? It'll be marvellous practice for you and it was you who said what a good story it would make when it all came out.'

'You mean, write down everything that happened in the right order, sort of thing?'

'Well, yes, that would be the bones of it, naturally, but I think you should aim to be creative, as well. You know, build up the personalities and so on. You met Rosamund McGrath, so you could start with a character sketch of her and then build up around it. You might do a series of interviews with some of the neighbours. That would also make a useful exercise.'

'Which neighbours?'

'Well, the Macadams, for a start. Louise always knows everything about everybody, so you'd pick up a lot from her and I'm sure she'll co-operate, if you explain that it's a serious project. And then there's Gregory Laycock. Doctors' opinions can often be valuable and he should be easy prey, now that you're going to be practically related.'

'Oh, don't remind me! Honestly, Tessa, I don't think I could bring myself to ask old Greg. He's such a creep!'

'Don't be so unprofessional. If you can't rise above your personal likes and dislikes, you'll never get anywhere.'

'Oh well, if you really think so, I suppose I might as well have a bash.'

'That's the spirit! And do remember not to be diffident about it, Millie. You'll get much more out of them, if you use shock tactics.'

On my return home from the christening, Robin informed me that Alan would be dining with us on the following Tuesday. Apparently, there had been some resistance to start with, but this had worn off when it was explained to him that two other guests would also be joining us. Robin had not thought it necessary to mention that they had been invited for eight o'clock.

'Oh, and by the way,' he added, 'I am afraid your informant was not so reliable as you supposed. No birth certificate for that name, date and place. You don't seem surprised.'

'I'm not.'

'Nor disappointed either?'

'No, it is what I expected. The thing was, I had to be sure, you see.'

'No, I don't see, far from it, but I suppose all will be revealed one day.'

'Which may not be far off now,' I assured him.

TWENTY-FIVE

'No, not a bit too early,' I said, pouring out the whisky and water. 'Robin has just telephoned to say he's on his way. Guy and Elizabeth are always late, but I expect they'll be here in a minute.'

Having impressed on Millie the value of shock tactics, I felt I could not do less than use them myself, so I sat down in the chair facing Alan and said:

'I'm afraid I'll have to leave you soon, to go and check on the dinner, but before I do there's something I want to ask you.'

He did not speak, but put his glass down and looked round the room, as though seeking some way to escape. So I went straight on, before he could find it:

'When, two years ago, Rosamund left you and went back to her husband, it wasn't because your wife had refused to divorce you, was it? That can't have come as any great surprise, so there must have been some other reason?'

Alan sighed and picked up his drink again. 'I suppose there would be no more point in denying it, since you seem to know so much, though how the hell . . .'

'By putting four and four together. And neither was it because, after all, she felt so rotten about stealing her dear cousin's husband that she found she couldn't go through with it?'

'No.'

'So would I be right in suggesting that, when it came to the crunch, she found the only thing she really wanted in life was a child? This had now become an obsession and more important to her than husband, cousin, lover, or any other man or woman. There were reasons why she couldn't have one of her own, in or out of wedlock and, anyway, she'd

180

probably left it too late by then, so it had to be adoption. She knew there wasn't a chance in the world of doing it legally, so long as she was living with a man she wasn't married to, so she repacked her bags and went back to the husband she'd already got. Isn't that how it was?'

'Yes.'

'And is it also true that after that fiasco you still continued to see each other and that, whatever your feelings, you were able to put up with the situation and revert to the status quo simply because she seemed to be getting nowhere with the adoption societies and you were sure that she would eventually accept defeat and give up the idea? But then one day she told you that it was all fixed. She had only to wait for the baby to be born and handed over to her. So that was that. It had been nice knowing you, but from now on you and she wouldn't be seeing each other any more. She'd be too busy, hiring nannies and turning one of the bedrooms into a nursery. Understandably, when that happened all your damped-down resentment and humiliation flared into rage and hatred and you . . .'

'That's enough!' he shouted, springing halfway out of the chair. 'I don't know what right you think you have to persecute me in this way, but I'm not taking any more, do you hear? I'll not stay here and listen to another word.'

'It's all right, Alan,' I said, hearing Robin's key in the front door and getting up too, 'no more questions. I've found out all I wanted to know.'

During dinner, which Alan had been obliged to forego, owing to a sudden onset of raging toothache, the telephone rang and I went into the kitchen to answer it.

'Sorry to pick such an awkward time,' Millie said, 'but I couldn't wait to tell you the news. The wedding's off!'

'No, really? Since when?'

'Since this afternoon. Marc came down to tell us. Andrea was supposed to have got mumps, but it wasn't true, apparently. She just wanted a few days on her own, to make up what she calls her mind and this afternoon he had a letter from her.'

'Well, congratulations!'

'Thanks. And the super thing is, Tessa, Marc doesn't seem all that bothered. I really think he's been getting more and more fed up with her lately. Ever since the inquest, in fact, so I suppose you were right there. Anyway, I thought you'd be pleased.'

'Yes, I'm delighted. And, by the way, Millie, how's the story coming along?'

'Oh, that! Well, to be brutally frank, it was a total flop.'

'Oh dear, what went wrong?'

'I started by tackling Tim and Louise, as you suggested. They were quite interested, in a patronising sort of way, but when I got down to the nitty gritty, like, you know, how they felt about living next door to a murderer and all that stuff, the whole atmosphere changed. It was awful, really, because Tim started twitching so furiously that I was afraid he would have a seizure. I think he may have been afraid he would too, because in the end he just got up and slammed out of the room.'

'And was that the end of it?'

'No, after that it was Louise's turn. She rounded on me and started ticking me off as though I was about four years old. And she kept asking me who'd put me up to it.'

'Did you tell her?'

'No, I said it was all my own idea and, anyway, I couldn't see what she was making such a fuss about. Then I slammed out too, so that wasn't a great success.'

'Did you try anyone else?'

'Yes, like you said, I had a go at Greg. That was yesterday, before we heard about Andrea, and it turned out even worse.'

'What happened?'

'He didn't lose his temper or anything, at least not so it showed. He was just frightfully rude and cutting and more or less told me to shove off. And you know what, Tessa? It was really weird because just as I was leaving he called me back and what do you think? He said "Who put you up to this?".'

'But you didn't tell him?'

'Yes, I did. I'd lost my nerve by then and I blamed it all on you. Sorry about that, but I'd sort of got to the end of my tether. I'm honestly beginning to wonder if I'm cut out for this job, after all.'

'Never mind, you'll be able to concentrate better, now that you've got the bridesmaid worry out of your life. And you're not doing badly at all. You've started shaking people out of their complacency, which is half the battle. I think you should try it out on Andrea next.'

'Andrea? My God, Tessa, what are you saying? I couldn't possibly.'

'I can't see why not. I presume she's back at home now, so she'll be alone there during the daytime. You could drop in tomorrow morning and toss out some remarks about how you hope you and she can go on being friends, even though you won't be sisters-in-law. That'll put her in your debt and you can ask her to help you with this job you've taken on. If it doesn't work, at least it'll be another lesson in how not to go about it.'

'Oh well, if you insist . . .'

'You can't expect it to be easy to start with, you know. You've got to learn as you go along. And, incidentally, Millie, if by any chance she should ask you who put you up to it, don't hesitate to tell her. It will be just what we need.'

TWENTY-SIX

'So you have pulled it off again,' Toby said, lowering the evening paper which Robin and I had brought with us from London and which included a report of the death by his own hand of an acquaintance of ours in a West End flat. 'And despite all the opposition! Congratulations!'

'Thanks, but I don't deserve them this time. So many people contributed so much that I can scarcely take any credit at all.'

'My dear Tessa, are you feeling quite well? You wouldn't care for some brandy to buck you up?'

'No, it's the truth. I was merely the clearing house where it all got sorted out. Alan, I need hardly say, was the prime exception. I don't know how often he purposely misled me, but everything he told me about the McGraths was coloured by his own sense of guilt. Otherwise, it was all constructive. You came up with the right guess more often than not and so did Robin, with his explanation for Alan's ambiguities. Even Louse did her share. By leaving out the endearments, she first put me on to the idea that Rosamund's letter was a forgery, which of course had been her intention all along.'

'I can't see how it helped you very much.'

'Oh, yes! Without that I should never have got to know James as I did, nor heard the story about coming home to find his wife had been murdered and spirited away. I should have had no part in what followed and his arrest would have meant nothing to me. Millie was a tremendous help too, in several ways, the first being the inquest. And it was she, you know, who broke through Andrea's defences and got her to talk about all the things she'd been trying to hide. Poor Andrea, she was always more sinned against than sinning, I believe.'

'Although the romancing and self-dramatisation had set in long before she had anything to hide,' Robin pointed out.

'Oh, I know, but just think what her life must have been with that monster of a father! Her mother died when she was born and he became both parents to her and a lot more besides. Ellen was right, as usual, when she said it verged on the incestuous. In his perverted way, he really was in love with Andrea and it took the form of keeping her virtually a prisoner. She couldn't escape, whichever way she turned, and it's no wonder that she often retreated into fantasy. The trouble was that it got mixed up with reality. She said what she wanted to believe and as soon as it was said she believed it. It ended with everyone thinking she was lying, even when she was speaking the truth.'

'And when did she ever do that, pray?'

'I can give you three instances. One was in her claim that her father hadn't told her that he would be home late on the night of the fire. Another was when she tried to tell the Coroner how she'd gone into the morning-room in an unsuccessful attempt to rescue her stepmother. He either didn't hear what she was saying, or considered it irrelevant, so she didn't get a hearing. Millie and I both assumed that she'd made it up, to show everyone what a heroine she was, but it wasn't quite like that. She really did go in, possibly just to show off, but what she did while she was there really was heroic, in its way. I should remind you that the curtains were blazing merrily by then. The light didn't extend as far as the spot where Mrs Laycock was lying, but it did illuminate the carpet round the bed and what do you think she saw? An empty gin bottle, in case you hadn't guessed. So she darted forward, whipped it up and stuffed it inside her dressing gown.'

'What did she want to do that for?' Toby asked.

'To protect her father. It was purely instinctive. She didn't at that moment, suspect him of murder, but she knew the bottle shouldn't be there and she still retained enough filial indoctrination to want to keep him out of trouble. All of

185

which explains how Gregory came to fluff his lines. He'd already told Louise that he'd seen the bottle on the bedside table, because he'd expected it still to be there when the fire had been put out. So he was prepared to be called upon to explain why his wife had been left alone in the house and also why she should have chosen to take a bottle of gin to bed with her, but the second part of the question never came and that threw him. He hadn't thought there was any risk attached to the Coroner knowing it had been there, because neither he nor Louise realised that he had any motive for making it easy for his wife to kill herself, but Andrea did.'

'Why?'

'She'd caught him at it before and that was the reason why she made up the story for Ellen's benefit about Mrs Laycock being a potential murderess and suicide case. And, incidentally, it wasn't only for Ellen's benefit, because although she claimed to be speaking in strictest confidence, she was actually doing so within earshot of half a dozen other people. Then the next day she seized the first opportunity to take it all back and pretend she'd only said those things because she was drunk. That was crafty and it had the desired effect, up to a point, but it still didn't do her any good. She'd picked the wrong one to confide in.'

'Just what motive did her father have, apart from the fact that the poor woman must have been a dreadful worry?'

'And an expensive one too. He'd only married her in the first place to provide himself with a housekeeper and a glorified nursery maid for Andrea. All that was over long ago and the situation was worsening every day. Keeping a nurse on the premises had cost him the earth, but at least it allowed him freedom. He'd lost that now and even more serious, from his point of view, was that the last cure really had worked. She was right off the drink and she was beginning to notice what was going on around her, which was something he couldn't afford. So, one way and another, it was time for her to go and she, poor creature, was the one to show him how to do it. He overheard the conversation she had with me at Elsa's dinner party and he took immediate steps to turn her dream into reality. At least, that was one of the suggestions I made when I went to see him and he didn't deny it.'

'You went to see him?'

'The day before yesterday, in his consulting room. I needn't have bothered really. After Millie's interview, when he learnt who had put her up to it, to use his own expression, I expect he'd already begun to realise that the game was up and Andrea's letter had clinched it for him.'

'Andrea wrote him a letter?'

'Oh, yes. Once she'd confessed everything to Millie, there was no longer any question of things going on as before. She's moved in with Elsa now, which is about the most sensible thing she's ever done in her life, but she left a letter behind for Gregory, telling him exactly what she had done and I think he had already decided what his way out was to be by the time I came knocking on his door. I suppose doctors are fortunate in that way,' I added, struck by a new thought. 'Unlike the rest of us, their daughters included, they know how to make suicide effective and easy for themselves at the same time.'

'What other suggestions did you put to him, while you were about it?' Robin asked, ignoring this digression.

'One was that, naturally, he could not risk getting the blaze started before Andrea had come home and gone to her room. Otherwise she might have noticed something which would have led to the fire brigade being called in too early. So, as soon as he came in himself, he went to say goodnight to his wife and put it to her that they should break the rules for once, and make sure she got a good night's sleep. In other words, he placed an opened bottle of gin on her bedside table. Then later, once he was sure that Andrea was tucked up in bed, he went to work with the cigarettes and matches. It never occurred to him, I might add, that she had been out with anyone but Marc, whom he had now graciously consented to accept as prospective son-in-law. He held no more brief for Marc than for any young man, but at least he was preferable to James McGrath.'

'You didn't tell us about Andrea's other lapse into truthfulness,' Toby said, 'or haven't I been listening?''

'That was when she was going on about wanting to become an actress and I wish now that I hadn't been so sharp with her, because it was sincere. She was tied by the leg, you see. She had no training, no qualifications and no money, except for those things her father wanted her to spend it on. All she had was looks and, in her dim way, she thought they would be enough. It was equally true when she told me the next day that it wasn't on, because her father had put his foot down. Poor Andrea, her life must have been hell. One escape would have been through marriage, but the prospects there weren't promising either, since all the eligible young men who came along were intimidated or shooed off by Gregory. Besides, the only man she wanted to marry was James, who already had a wife whom he had no intention of abandoning.'

Robin said: 'Before we all get too sorry for her, I ought to remind you that she certainly strayed from the truth when she told your reliable informant that she'd had a child two years ago in Newquay.'

'I know, and that's what I meant by getting fantasy and reality mixed up. It didn't happen two years ago, but something very like it should have happened next winter or early spring.'

They both looked at me as though I had gone mad and I explained:

'Three or four months ago Andrea discovered that she was pregnant. James was the father, of course. He was the only man she'd ever loved and she did it deliberately, as a last throw to get him for herself. As soon as the tests were pronounced positive, she went to see Rosamund and threw herself on her mercy. She told her that she and James had been in love for years and, now that she was going to have the child which Rosamund couldn't or wouldn't give him, she

188

was begging her to do the noble thing and release him.'

'Which sent Rosamund into gales of laugher and ruined the act; whereupon Andrea picked up the carving knife and stabbed her through the heart?' Toby suggested.

'Not at all, she offered Andrea a deal. She said that, if she were to consent to a divorce, it would have to be on her own terms. Andrea was to go away somewhere for five or six months and have the baby. Rosamund would make all the arrangements and pay all the expenses for this, as well as for a private confinement. As soon as the child was born, presuming it to be normal and healthy, Andrea would relinquish all claim and it would, be handed over to Rosamund, who would then begin the process of legal adoption. The day this was completed, she would file a suit for divorce, on grounds of adultery, for which she already had all the evidence she needed. Andrea's name would not be brought into it and she and James would be free to marry and have as many children as they thought proper. Pretty cunning, don't you think? A true case of having her cake and eating it.'

'And Andrea agreed?'

'Not only agreed, but told her father what she was planning to do. She had no alternative, of course, but it must have taken courage.'

'And he, I presume, was not best pleased?'

'That is even more of an understatement than you intended it to be, Toby. He behaved like a madman, ranting and raging, sobbing and entreating; using every trick in the book, short of physical assault. She still wouldn't give in, though, and of course he couldn't force her to have an abortion. For one thing, she might have told the gynaecologist that she secretly wanted to keep the baby, in which case he'd have refused to go on with it.'

'Although obviously she did have one, otherwise we'd have noticed something by now.'

'Yes, I don't know how long she would have stood out, but she was never put to the test. It was only a few weeks later

189

that the stories about Rosamund's disappearance began to get around. James told her she had run off with another man and that sent the whole plan up in smoke. She knew that no one would be able to adopt a child legally in those circumstances. So she gave in, had the abortion and became a good little daughter again. It affected her deeply, though, and there was worse to come.'

'Oh dear, how sad! I don't know if I can stand any more.'

'You must steel yourself, Toby, because when the weeks went by, with still no word from Rosamund, the local gossips began hinting that James had murdered her and buried the remains in the garden. That was when Andrea got her first glimmer of what might really have happened and who had been responsible. Naturally, she couldn't speak of it to anyone, least of all James, and so it was then that she took to fantasising on the grand scale and also when she became so desperate to escape. She would have done anything, got any sort of job, married Marc, whom she didn't care for in the least, to get out of her father's clutches. Curiously enough, it was he who put her on the first step to doing so.'

'By encouraging her to go jaunting off to the Hebrides?' Robin suggested.

'Persuading her to, in fact. The fire had been the last straw, you see. It is true that she acted instinctively at the time, but afterwards and during the inquest she became obsessed with the idea that her father was guilty of that crime as well. Which, of course, only strengthened her belief that he had committed the first one. Gregory could see that she was at breaking point and was scared silly of what she might say or do. So he persuaded her to pack her bags and take a little holiday.'

'And where did she actually go?'

'To some crummy hotel in Kensington. She sold all her jewellery and trekked around the employment agencies. She was hoping to get a job as a stewardess on an ocean liner, if you can believe such a thing? Poor Andrea!'

'But they wouldn't take her and so she came back?'

'No, Toby, she came back when she heard the dead woman in Herefordshire had been identified. How could she contemplate leaving the country, knowing that James would stand trial for a crime which she had reason to believe her own father had committed? She came back and once again she turned to Marc as her last resort, but it didn't take her long to discover that she couldn't go through with it. There was really no way out for the wretched girl and in the end I believe it came as a relief to pour it all out to Millie.'

Toby said: 'You have explained it all so well that I think I understand, so far as one can ever understand such behaviour, but one thing still puzzles me. Why, having killed someone, should it be necessary to go to the trouble of wrapping her in a sheet and carting her away? Why not leave her where she was?'

'There were a number of reasons, and the first thing to remember is that killing her was not enough. It had to be done, to prevent her from taunting and humiliating him for the rest of his life with the knowledge that she was bringing up his illegitimate grandchild, but James had to pay the price too, for seducing his beloved daughter.'

'Surely, leaving Rosamund where she was would have made certain of that?'

'No, by removing her to a place associated with James, he first of all ensured that enough time would pass to make it impossible to establish the day, or, with luck, the week of her death. This would be an advantage to him, but no help to James. Secondly, he couldn't be certain that James would have no alibi for the time when death, in fact, did occur. The Macadams were away, as he knew so well, since it was an essential part of his plan to eliminate the risk of being seen by them, himself, that morning. But there was still the outside chance that James could have come across someone while he was up in the woods. Finally, there was no guarantee that James would inform the police of what had happened. He could well have reasoned that his best bet would be to wrap Rosamund in a sheet himself, and take her

191

to a place where she might never be found. That would have ruined everything.'

'Although you could say that it was only by a fluke that she was found in the place which Gregory had chosen?'

'Oh no, it was on private land and it would have happened sooner or later, probably as soon as the owners returned and went to see how their larch grove was coming along.'

'So what will Andrea do now, poor thing?'

'Marry James, of course, and have as many children as they think proper. That is, if he'll have her and I hope he will. She deserves to get what she wants for once in her life and it certainly won't cause Rosamund to turn in her grave.'

As I spoke, the telephone rang, causing Toby to shudder:

'So it has started already! It will save time if you answer it yourself.'

'It was my agent,' I announced. 'The L.A. deal is off. The union is kicking up a fuss and insisting on an American actress for the part. She'll never get the accent right, but what do they care?'

'I am disappointed,' Toby said. 'I had been looking forward to sixteen weeks of blessed peace and quiet.'

'Cheer up!' Robin told him. 'At least, you won't be woken up at three in the morning by all those transatlantic telephone calls from someone who can never remember whether the time goes back or forward.'

'Besides, who wants peace and quiet, so long as we have murderers in our midst? Personally, I feel relieved to have the decision taken out of my hands. How about you, Robin?'

'Oh, I am delighted. I'm another who doesn't care for being woken up at three in the morning. Besides, I'm too old a dog to start learning new tricks now. Peace and quiet would take a bit of getting used to.'